The Alliance is plagued by a series of devastating attacks. Each unpredictable, each preceded by a message in Babel-17, the Invaders' mysterious battle-code. Only Rydra Wong, a gifted poet and linguist, mistress of a thousand tongues, can fathom its perilous secret. Her quest takes her across half the galaxy, and brings her together with a bizarre company:

BRASS: Wrestler and star-pilot genetically altered, with muscles of steel and nerves of quicksilver.

CALLI, RON and MOLLYA: Navigators; a "triple" who find love and trust on a dangerous mission.

BARON VER DORCO: Armorer for the alliance, weapons master for a galaxy, who created an ultimate weapon he could not control . . . and

THE BUTCHER: Fugitive, murderer, pirate, lover, who holds the deepest secret of Babel-17.

A thrilling adventure of intricate invention.

BABEL-17

Bantam Books by Samuel R. Delany
Ask your bookseller for the books you have missed

BABEL-17
DHALGREN
DISTANT STARS
NOVA
TALES OF NEVÈRYÖN
TRITON

BABEL-17

Samuel R. Delany

BANTAM BOOKS
TORONTO · NEW YORK · LONDON · SYDNEY

BABEL-17

*A Bantam Book / published by arrangement with
the Author*

PRINTING HISTORY
Sphere Books published 1969
Gregg Press edition published 1976
Bantam edition / February 1982

*All epigraphs are from poems by Marilyn Hacker. Most of those
excerpted here were later included in her collections Presentation
Piece (by Marilyn Hacker, Viking Press; New York, 1974) and
Separations (by Marilyn Hacker, Alfred A. Knopf; New York,
1976). A few lines here are earlier versions of those to be found in
the volume collections.*

ISBN 0-553-20156-5

Published simultaneously in the United States and Canada

---

*Bantam Books are published by Bantam Books, Inc. Its trade-
mark, consisting of the words "Bantam Books" and the por-
trayal of a rooster, is Registered in U.S. Patent and Trademark
Office and in other countries. Marca Registrada. Bantam
Books, Inc., 666 Fifth Avenue, New York, New York 10103.*

PRINTED IN THE UNITED STATES OF AMERICA

0 9 8 7 6 5 4 3 2 1

*—this one, now, is
for Bob Folsom,
to explain just a little of
the past year—*

NOTE ON THE TEXT
OF THIS EDITION

For this edition Bantam Books has kindly allowed me to restore certain typographical complexities, included in the original manuscript, that fifteen years ago Babel-17's initial publisher was unable to include for technical reasons. As well, some extremely minor cuts have been restored, for all of which I am appropriately grateful.

—S. R. DELANY

PART ONE

~~~~~~

Rydra Wong

...Here is the hub of ambiguity.
Electric spectra splash across the street.
Equivocation knots the shadowed features
of boys who are not boys; a quirk of darkness
shrivels a full mouth to senility
or pares it to a razor-edge, pours acid
across an amber cheek, fingers
a crotch, or smashes in the pelvic arch
and wells a dark clot oozing in a chest
dispelled with motion or a flare of light
that swells the lips and dribbles them with blood.
They say the hustlers paint their lips with blood.
They say the same crowd surges up the street
and surges down again, like driftwood borne
tidewise ashore and sucked away with backwash,
only to slap into the sand again,
only to be jerked out and spun away.
Driftwood; the narrow hips, the liquid eyes,
the wideflung shoulders and the rough-cast hands,
the gray-faced jackals kneeling to their prey.

The colors disappear at break of day
when stragglers toward the west riverdocks meet
young sailors ambling shipward on the street . . .

—from *Prism and Lens*.

1

It's a port city.

Here fumes rust the sky, the General thought. Industrial gases flushed the evening with oranges, salmons, purples with too much red. West, ascending and descending transports, shuttling cargoes to stellarcenters and satellites, lacerated the clouds. It's a rotten poor city too, thought the General, turning the corner by the garbage-strewn curb.

Since the Invasion six ruinous embargoes for months apiece had strangled this city whose lifeline must pulse with interstellar commerce to survive. Sequestered, how could this city exist? Six times in twenty years he'd asked himself that. Answer? It couldn't.

Panics, riots, burnings, twice cannibalism—

The General looked from the silhouetted loading-towers that jutted behind the rickety monorail to the grimy buildings. The streets were smaller here, cluttered with transport workers, loaders, a few stellarmen in green uniforms, and the hoard of pale, proper men and women who managed the intricate sprawl of customs operations. They are quiet now, intent on home or work, the General thought. Yet all these people have lived for two decades under the Invasion. They've starved during the embargoes, broken windows, looted, run screaming before firehoses, torn flesh from a corpse's arm with decalcified teeth.

Who is this animal man? He asked himself the abstract question to blur the lines of memory. It was easier, being a general, to ask about the "animal man" than about the woman who had sat in the middle of the sidewalk during the last

3

embargo holding her skeletal baby by one leg, or the three scrawny teen-age girls who had attacked him on the street with razors (—she had hissed through brown teeth, the bar of metal glistening towards his chest, "Come here, Beefsteak! Come get me, Lunch-meat . . ." He had used karate—) or the blind man who had walked up the avenue, screaming.

Pale and proper men and women now, who spoke softly, who always hesitated before they let an expression fix their faces, with pale, proper, patriotic ideas: work for victory over the Invaders; Alona Star and Kip Rhyak were great in "Stellar Holliday" but Ronald Quar was the best serious actor around. They listened to Hi Lite's music (or did they listen, wondered the General, during those slow dances where no one touched). A position in Customs was a good secure job.

Working directly in Transport was probably more exciting and fun to watch in the movies; but really, such strange people—

Those with more intelligence and sophistication discussed Rydra Wong's poetry.

They spoke of the Invasion often, with some hundred phrases consecrated by twenty years' repetition on newscasts and in the papers. They referred to the embargoes seldom, and only by the one word.

Take any of them, take any million. Who are they? What do they want? What would they say if given a chance to say anything?

Rydra Wong has become this age's voice. The General recalled the glib line from a hyperbolic review. Paradoxical: a military leader with a military goal, he was going to meet Rydra Wong now.

The street lights came on and his image glazed on the plate glass window of the bar. That's right, I'm not wearing my uniform now. He saw a tall, muscular man with the authority of half a century in his craggy face. He was uncomfortable in the gray civilian suit. Till age thirty, the physical impression he had left with people was "big and bumbling." Afterwards—the change had coincided with the Invasion—it was "massive and authoritarian."

Had Rydra Wong come to see him at Administrative

Alliance Headquarters, he would have felt secure. But he was in civvies, not in stellarman-green. The bar was new to him. And she was the most famous poet in five explored galaxies. For the first time in a long while he felt bumbling again.

He went inside.

And whispered, "My God, she's beautiful," without even having to pick her from among the other women. "I didn't know she was so beautiful, not from the pictures. . . ."

She turned to him (as the figure in the mirror behind the counter caught sight of him and turned away), stood up from the stool, smiled.

He walked forward, took her hand, the words *Good evening, Miss Wong*, tumbling on his tongue till he swallowed them unspoken. And now she was about to speak.

She wore copper lipstick, and the pupils of her eyes were beaten disks of copper—

"Babel-17," she said. "I haven't solved it yet, General Forester."

A knitted indigo dress, and her hair like fast water at night spilling one shoulder; he said, "That doesn't really surprise us, Miss Wong."

Surprise, he thought. She puts her hand on the bar, she leans back on the stool, hip moving in knitted blue, and with each movement, I am amazed, surprised, bewildered. Can I be this off guard, or can she really be that—

"But I've gotten further than you people at Military have been able to." The gentle line of her mouth bowed with gentler laughter.

"From what I've been led to expect of you, Miss Wong, that doesn't surprise me either." Who is she? he thought. He had asked the question of the abstract population. He had asked it of his own reflected image. He asked it of her now, thinking, No one else matters, but I must know about her. That's important. I have to know.

"First of all, General," she was saying, "Babel-17 isn't a code."

His mind skidded back to the subject and arrived teetering. "Not a code? But I thought Cryptography had at least established——" He stopped, because he wasn't sure what Cryptography had established, and because he needed another moment to haul himself down from the ledges of her high cheekbones, to retreat from the caves of her eyes. Tightening the muscles of his face, he marshaled his thoughts to Babel -17. The Invasion: Babel-17 might be one key to ending this twenty-year scourge. "You mean we've just been trying to decipher a lot of nonsense?"

"It's not a code," she repeated. "It's a language."

The General frowned. "Well, whatever you call it, code or language, we still have to figure out what it says. As long as we don't understand it, we're a hell of a way from where we should be." The exhaustion and pressure of the last months homed in his belly, a secret beast to strike the back of his tongue, harshening his words.

Her smile had left, and both hands were on the counter. He wanted to retract the harshness. She said, "You're not directly connected with the Cryptography Department." The voice was even, calming.

He shook his head.

"Then let me tell you this. Basically, General Forester, there are two types of codes, ciphers, and true codes. In the first, letters, or symbols that stand for letters, are shuffled and juggled according to a pattern. In the second, letters, words, or groups of words are replaced by other letters, symbols, or words. A code can be one type or the other, or a combination. But both have this in common: once you find the key, you just plug it in and out come logical sentences. A language, however, has its own internal logic, its own grammar, its own way of putting thoughts together with words that span various spectra of meaning. There is no key you can plug in to unlock the exact meaning. At best you can get a close approximation."

"Do you mean that Babel-17 decodes into some other language?"

"Not at all. That's the first thing I checked. We can take a probability scan on various elements and see if they are congruent with other language patterns, even if these elements are in the wrong order. No. Babel-17 is a language itself which we do not understand."

"I think"—General Forester tried to smile—"what you're trying to tell me is that because it isn't a code, but rather an alien language, we might as well give up." If this were defeat, receiving it from her was almost relief.

But she shook her head. "I'm afraid that's not what I'm saying at all. Unknown languages have been deciphered without translations, Linear B and Hittite for example. But if I'm to get further with Babel-17, I'll have to know a great deal more."

The General raised his eyebrows. "What more do you need to know? We've given you all our samples. When we get more, we'll certainly——"

"General, I have to know everything you know about Babel-17; where you got it, when, under what circumstances, anything that might give me a clue to the subject matter."

"We've released all the information that we——"

"You gave me ten pages of double-spaced typewritten garble with the code name Babel-17 and asked me what it meant. With just that I can't tell you. With more, I might. It's that simple."

He thought: If it were that simple, if it were only that simple, we would never have called you in about it, Rydra Wong.

She said: "If it were that simple, if it were only that simple, you would never have called me in about it, General Forester."

He started, for one absurd moment convinced she had read his mind. But of course, she would know that. Wouldn't she?

"General Forester, has your Cryptography Department even discovered it's a language?"

"If they have, they haven't told me."

"I'm fairly sure they don't know. I've made a few structural inroads on the grammar. Have they done that?"

"No."

"General, although they know a hell of a lot about codes, they know nothing of the nature of language. That sort of idiotic specialization is one of the reasons I haven't worked with them for the past six years."

Who is she? he thought again. A security dossier had been handed him that morning, but he had passed it to his aide and merely noted, later, that it had been marked "ap-

proved.'' He heard himself say, ''Perhaps if you could tell me
a little about yourself, Miss Wong, I could speak more freely
with you.'' Illogical, yet he'd spoken it with measured calm
and surety. Was her expression quizzical?

''What do you want to know?''

''What I already know is only this: your name, and that
some time ago you worked for Military Cryptography. I know
that even though you left when very young, you had enough
of a reputation so that, six years laer, the people who
remembered you said unanimously—after they had struggled
with Babel-17 for a month—'Send it to Rydra Wong.' '' He
paused. ''And you tell me you have gotten someplace with it.
So they were right.''

''Let's have drinks,'' she said.

The bartender drifted forward, drifted back, leaving two
small glasses of smoky green. She sipped, watching him. Her
eyes, he thought, slant like astounded wings.

''I'm not from Earth,'' she said. ''My father was a
Communications engineer at Stellarcenter X-11-B just beyond
Uranus. My mother was a translator for the Court of Outer
Worlds. Until I was seven I was the spoiled brat of the
Stellarcenter. There weren't many children. We moved rock-
side to Uranus-XXVII in '52. By the time I was twelve, I
knew seven Earth languages and could make myself understood in five extra-terrestrial tongues. I pick up languages like
most people pick up the lyrics to popular songs. I lost both
parents during the second embargo.''

''You were on Uranus during the embargo?''

''You know what happened?''

''I know the Outer Planets were hit a lot harder than the
Inner.''

''You don't know. But yes, they were.'' She drew a
breath as memory surprised her. ''One drink isn't enough to
make me talk about it, though. When I came out of the
hospital, there was a chance I may have had brain damage.''

''Brain damage——?''

''Malnutrition you know about. Add neuro-sciatic plague.''

''I know about plague, too.''

''Anyway, I came to Earth to stay with an aunt and uncle
here and receive neuro-therapy. Only I didn't need it. And I

don't know whether it was psychological or physiological, but I came out of the whole business with total verbal recall. I'd been bordering on it all my life so it wasn't too odd. But I also had perfect pitch.''

"Doesn't that usually go along with lightning calculation and eidetic memory? I can see how all of them would be of use to a cryptographer.''

"I'm a good mathematician, but no lightning calculator. I test high on visual conception and special relations—dream in technicolor and all that—but the total recall is strictly verbal. I had already begun writing. During the summer I got a job translating with the government and began to bone up on codes. In a little while I discovered that I had a certain knack. I'm not a good cryptographer. I don't have the patience to work that hard on anything written down that I didn't write myself. Neurotic as hell; that's another reason I gave it up for poetry. But the 'knack' was sort of frightening. Somehow, when I had too much work to do, and somewhere else I really wanted to be, and was scared my supervisor would start getting on my neck, suddenly everything I knew about communication would come together in my head, and it was easier to read the thing in front of me and say what it said than to be that scared and tired and miserable.''

She glanced at her drink.

"Eventually the knack almost got to where I could control it. By then I was nineteen and had a reputation as the little girl who could crack anything. I guess it was knowing something about language that did it, being more facile at recognizing patterns—like distinguishing grammatical order from random rearrangement by feel, which is what I did with Babel-17.''

"Why did you leave?''

"I've given you two reasons. A third is simply that when I mastered the knack, I wanted to use it for my own purposes. At nineteen, I quit the Military and, well, got . . . married, and started writing seriously. Three years later my first book came out.'' She shrugged, smiled. "For anything after that, read the poems. It's all there.''

"And on the worlds of five galaxies, now, people delve your imagery and meaning for the answers to the riddles of

language, love, and isolation." The three words jumped his
sentence like vagabonds on a boxcar. She was before him,
and was talking; here, divorced from the military, he felt
desperately isolated; and he was desperately in——No!

That was impossible and ridiculous and too simple to
explain what coursed and pulsed behind his eyes, inside his
hands. "Another drink?" Automatic defense. But she will
take it for automatic politeness. Will she? The bartender
came, left.

"The worlds of five galaxies," she repeated. "That's so
strange. I'm only twenty-six." Her eyes fixed somewhere
behind the mirror. She was only half through her first drink.

"By the time Keats was your age, he was dead."

She shrugged. "This is an odd epoch. It takes heroes
very suddenly, very young, then drops them as quickly."

He nodded, recalling half a dozen singers, actors, even
writers in their late teens or early twenties who had been
named genius for a year, two, three, only to disappear. Her
reputation was only a phenomenon of three years' duration.

"I'm part of my times," she said. "I'd like to transcend
my times, but the times themselves have a good deal to do
with who I am." Her hand retreated across the mahogany
from her glass. "You in Military, it must be much the
same." She raised her head. "Have I given you what you
want?"

He nodded. It was easier to lie with a gesture than a
word.

"Good. Now, General Forester, what's Babel-17?"

He looked around for the bartender, but a glow brought
his eyes back to her face: the glow was simply her smile, but
from the corner of his eye he had actually mistaken it for a
light. "Here," she said, pushing her second drink, untouched,
to him. "I won't finish this."

He took it, sipped. "The Invasion, Miss Wong . . . it's
got to be involved with the Invasion."

She leaned on one arm, listening with narrowing eyes.

"It started with a series of accidents—well, at first they
seemed like accidents. Now we're sure it's sabotage. They've
occurred all over the Alliance regularly since December '68.
Some on warships, some in Space Navy Yards, usually

involving the failure of some important equipment. Twice, explosions have caused the death of important officials. Several times these 'accidents' have happened in industrial plants producing essential war products.''

"What connects all these 'accidents', other than that they touched on the war? With our economy working this way, it would be difficult for any major industrial accident not to affect the war.''

"The thing that connects them all, Miss Wong, is Babel-17.''

He watched her finish her drink and set the glass precisely on the wet circle.

"Just before, during, and immediately after each accident, the area is flooded with radio exchanges back and forth from indefinite sources; most of them only have a carrying power of a couple of hundred yards. But there are occasional bursts through hyperstatic channels that blanket a few light-years. We have transcribed the stuff during the last three 'accidents' and given it the working title Babel-17. Now. Does that tell you anything you can use?''

"Yes. There's a good chance you're receiving radio instructions for the sabotage back and forth between whatever is directing the 'accidents'——''

"—But we can't find a thing!'' Exasperation struck. "There's nothing but that blasted gobbledy-gook, piping away at double speed! Finally someone noticed certain repetitions in the pattern that suggested a code. Cryptography seemed to think it was a good lead but couldn't crack it for a month; so they called you.''

As he talked, he watched her think. Now she said, "General Forester, I'd like the original monitors of these radio exchanges, plus a thorough report, second by second if it's available, of those accidents timed to the tapes.''

"I don't know if——''

"If you don't have such a report, make one during the next 'accident' that occurs. If this radio garbage is a conversation, I have to be able to follow what's being talked about. You may not have noticed, but, in the copy Cryptography gave me, there was no distinction as to which voice was which. In short, what I'm working with now is a transcription of a highly technical exchange run together without punctuation, or even word breaks.''

''I can probably get you everything you want except the original recordings——''

''You have to. I must make my own transcription, carefully, and on my own equipment.''

''We'll make a new one to your specifications.''

She shook her head. ''I have to do it myself, or I can't promise a thing. There's the whole problem of phonemic and allophonic distinctions. Your people didn't even realize it was a language, so it didn't occur to them——''

Now he interrupted her. ''*What* sort of distinctions?''

''You know the way some Orientals confuse the sounds of R and L when they speak a Western language? That's because R and L in many Eastern languages are allophones, that is, considered the same sound, written and even heard the same—just like the *th* at the beginning of *they* and at the beginning of *theater*.''

''What's different about the sound of *th*eatre and *th*ey?''

''Say them again and listen. One's voiced and the other's unvoiced, they're as distinct as V and F; only they're allophones—at least in British English; so Britishers are used to hearing them as though they were the same phoneme. Now Americans, of course, have the minimal pair 'ether/either,' where the voicing alone marks the semantic difference—''

''Oh . . .''

''But you see the problem a 'foreigner' has transcribing a language he doesn't speak; he may come out with too many distinctions of sound, or not enough.''

''How do you propose to do it?''

''By what I know about the sound systems of a lot of other languages and by feel.''

''The 'knack' again?''

She smiled. ''I suppose.''

She waited for him to grant approval. What wouldn't he have granted her? For a moment he had been distracted by her voice through subtleties of sound. ''Of course, Miss Wong,'' he said, ''you're our expert. Come to Cryptography tomorrow and you can have access to whatever you need.''

"Thank you, General Forester. I'll bring my official report in then."

He stood in the static beam of her smile. I must go now, he thought desperately. Oh, let me say something more— "Fine, Miss Wong. I'll speak to you then." Something more, something—

He wrenched his body away. (I must turn from her.) Say one thing more, thank you, be you, love you. He walked to the door, his thoughts quieting: who is she? Oh, the things that should have been said. I have been brusque, military, efficient. But the luxurience of thought and word I would have given her. The door swung open and evening brushed blue fingers on his eyes.

My god, he thought, as coolness struck his face, all that inside me and she doesn't know! I didn't communicate a thing! Somewhere in the depths the words, *not a thing, you're still safe*. But stronger on the surface was the outrage at his own silence. Didn't communicate a thing at all——

Rydra stood up, her hands on the edge of the counter, looking at the mirror. The bartender came to remove the glasses at her fingertips. As he reached for them, he frowned.

"Miss Wong?"

Her face was fixed.

"Miss Wong, are you——"

Her knuckles were white, and as the bartender watched, the whiteness crept along her hands till they looked like shaking wax.

"Is there something wrong, Miss Wong?"

She snapped her face toward him. "You noticed?" Her voice was a hoarse whisper, harsh, sarcastic, strained. She whirled from the bar and started toward the door, stopped once to cough, then hurried on.

II

~~~~~~

"Mocky, help me!"

"Rydra?" Dr. Markus T'mwarba pushed himself from
the pillow in the darkness. Her face sprung in smoky light
above the bed. "Where are you?"

"Downstairs, Mocky. Please, I've got to talk to you."
Her agitated features moved right, left, trying to avoid his
look. He squinched his eyes against the glare, then opened
them slowly. "Come on up."

Her face disappeared.

He waved his hand across the control board, and soft
light filled the sumptuous bedroom. He shoved back the gold
quilt, stood on the fur rug, took a black silk robe from a
gnarled bronze column, and as he swung it across his back
the automatic contour wires wrapped the panels across his
chest and straightened the shoulders. He brushed the induc-
tion bank in the rococo frame again, and aluminium flaps fell
back on the sideboard. A steaming carafe and liquor decant-
ers rolled forward.

Another gesture started bubble chairs inflating from the
floor. As Dr. T'mwarba turned to the entrance cabinet,
it creaked, mica wings slid out, and Rydra caught her
breath.

"Coffee?" He pushed the carafe and the force-field
caught it and carried it gently toward her. "What've you been
doing?"

"Mocky, it . . . I . . . ?"

"Drink your coffee."

She poured a cup, lifted it halfway to her mouth. "No sedatives?"

"Crème de cacao or crème de cafe?" He held up two small glasses. "Unless you think alcohol is cheating, too. Oh, and there're some franks and beans left over from dinner. I had company."

She shook her head. "Just cacao."

The tiny glass followed the coffee across the beam. "I've had a perfectly dreadful day." He folded his hands. "No work all afternoon, dinner guests who wanted to argue, and then deluged with calls from the moment they left. Just got to sleep ten minutes ago." He smiled. "How was your evening?"

"Mocky, it . . . it was terrible."

Dr. T'mwarba sipped his liqueur. "Good. Otherwise I'd never forgive you for waking me up."

In spite of herself she smiled. "I can . . . can always c-c-count on you for s-sympathy, Mocky."

"You can count on me for good sense and cogent psychiatric advice. Sympathy? I'm sorry, not after eleven-thirty. Sit down. What happened?" A final sweep of his hand brought a chair up behind her. The edge tapped the back of her knees and she sat. "Now stop stuttering and talk to me. You got over that when you were fifteen." His voice had become very gentle and very sure.

She took another sip of coffee. "The code, you remember the code I was working on?"

Dr. T'mwarba lowered himself to a wide leather hammock and brushed back his white hair, still awry from sleep. "I remember you were asked to work on something for the government. You were rather scornful of the business."

"Yes. And . . . well, it's not the code—which is a language, by the way—but just this evening, I-I talked to the General in charge, General Forester, and it happened . . . I mean again, it happened, and I knew!"

"Knew what?"

"Just like last time, knew what he was thinking!"

"You read his mind?"

"No. No, it was just like last time! I could tell, from what he was doing, what he was saying . . ."

"You've tried to explain this to me before, but I still don't understand, unless you're talking about some sort of telepathy."

She shook her head, shook it again.

Dr. T'mwarba locked his fingers and leaned back. Suddenly Rydra said in an even voice: *"Now I do have some idea of what you're trying to say, dear, but you'll have to put it in words yourself.* That's what you were about to say, Mocky, wasn't it?"

T'mwarba raised the white hedges of his eyebrows. "Yes. It was. You say you didn't read my mind? You've demonstrated this to me a dozen times——"

"I know what *you're* trying not to say; and you don't know what *I'm* trying to say. It's not fair!" She nearly rose from her seat.

They said in unison: "That's why you're such a fine poet." Rydra went on, "I know, Mocky. I have to work things out carefully in my head and put them in my poems so people will understand. But that's not what I've been doing for the past ten years. You know what I do? I listen to other people, stumbling about with their half thoughts and half sentences and their clumsy feelings that they can't express, and it hurts me. So I go home and burnish it and polish it and weld it to a rhythmic frame, make the dull colors gleam, mute the garish artificiality to pastels, so it doesn't hurt any more: that's my poem. I know what they want to say, and I say it for them."

"The voice of your age," said T'mwarba.

She said something unprintable. When she finished there were tears starting on her lower lids. "What *I* want to say, what I want to express, *I* just . . ." Again she shook her head. "I can't say it."

"If you want to keep growing as a poet, you'll have to."

She nodded. "Mocky, up till a year ago, I didn't even realize I was just saying other people's ideas. I thought they were my own."

"Every young writer who's worth anything goes through that. That's when you learn your craft."

"And now I have things to say that are all my own. They're not what other people have said before, put in an original way. And they're not just violent contradictions of what other people have said, which amounts to the same thing. They're new, and I'm scared to death."

"Every young writer who becomes a mature writer has to go through that."

"It's easy to repeat; it's hard to speak, Mocky."

"Good, if you're learning that now. Why don't you start by telling me exactly how this...this business of your understanding works?"

She was silent for five, stretching to ten, seconds. "All right. I'll try again. Just before I left the bar, I was standing there, looking in the mirror, and the bartender came up and asked me what was wrong."

"Could he sense you were upset?"

"He didn't 'sense' anything. He looked at my hands. They were clenched on the edge of the bar and they were turning white. He didn't have to be a genius to figure out something odd was going on in my head."

"Bartenders are pretty sensitive to that sort of signal. It's part of their job." He finished his coffee. "Your fingers were turning white? All right, what was this General saying to you, or not saying to you, that he wanted to say?"

A muscle in her cheek jumped twice, and Dr. T'mwarba thought, Should I be able to interpret that more specifically than just her nervousness?

"He was a brisk, ramrod efficient man," she explained, "probably unmarried, with a military career, and all the insecurity that implies. He was in his fifties, and feeling odd about it. He walked into the bar where we were supposed to meet; his eyes narrowed, then opened, his hand was resting against his leg, and the fingers suddenly curled, then straightened, his pace slowed as he came in, but quickened by the time he was three steps toward me, and he shook my hand like he was afraid it would break."

T'mwarba's smile turned into laughter. "He fell in love with you!"

She nodded.

"But why in the world should that upset you? I think you should be flattered."

"Oh, I was!" She leaned forward. "I *was* flattered. And I could follow the whole thing through his head. Once, when he was trying to get his mind back on the code, Babel-17, I said exactly what he was thinking, just to let him know I was so close to him. I watched the thought go by that perhaps I was reading his mind——"

"Wait a minute. This is the part I don't understand. How did you know *exactly* what he was thinking?"

She raised her hand to her jaw. "He told me, here. I said something about needing more information to crack the language. He didn't want to give it to me. I said I had to have it or I couldn't get any farther, it was that simple. He raised his head just a fraction—to avoid shaking it. If he had shaken his head, with a slight pursing of the lips, what do you think he would have been saying?"

Dr. T'mwarba shrugged. "That it wasn't as simple as you thought?"

"Yes. Now he made one gesture to avoid making that one. What does that mean?"

T'mwarba shook his head.

"He avoided the gesture because he connected its not being that simple with my being there. So he raised his head instead."

"Something like: If it were that simple, we wouldn't need you," T'mwarba suggested.

"Exactly. Now, while he raised his head, there was a slight pause halfway up. Don't you see what that adds?"

"No."

"If it were that simple—now the pause—if *only* it were that simple, we wouldn't have called you in about it." She turned her hands up in her lap. "And I said it back to him; then his jaw clenched——"

"In surprise?"

"—Yes. That's when he wondered for a second if I could read his mind."

Dr. T'mwarba shook his head. "It's too exact, Rydra. What you're describing is muscle-reading, which can be pretty accurate, especially if you know the logical area the person's thoughts are centred on. But it's still too exact. Get back to why you were upset by the business. Your modesty was offended by the attention of this . . . uncouth stellarman?"

She came back with something neither modest nor couth.

Dr. T'mwarba bit the inside of his lip and wondered if she saw.

"I'm not a little girl," she said. "Besides, he wasn't thinking anything uncouth. As I said, I was flattered by the whole thing. When I pulled my little joke, I was just trying to let him know how much in key we were. I thought he was charming. And if he had been able to see as clearly as I could he would have known I had nothing but good feeling for him. Only when he left——"

Dr. T'mwarba heard roughness work back into her voice.

"——when he left, the last thing he thought was, 'She doesn't know; I haven't communicated a thing to her.' "

Her eyes darkened—no, she bent slightly forward and half dropped her upper lids so that her eyes looked darker. He had watched that happen thousands of times since the scrawny near-autistic twelve-year-old girl had been sent to him for neurotherapy, which had developed into psychotherapy, and then into friendship. This was the first time he'd understood the mechanics of the effect. Her precision of observation had inspired him before to look more closely at others. Only since therapy had officially ended had it come full circle and made him look more closely at her. What did the darkening signify other than change? He knew there were myriad marks of personality about him that she read with a microscope. Wealthy, worldly, he had known many people equal to her in reputation. The reputation did not awe him. Often she did.

"He thought I didn't understand. He thought nothing had been communicated. And I was angry. I was hurt. All the misunderstandings that tie the world up and keep people apart were quivering before me at once, waiting for me to untangle them, explain them, and I couldn't. I didn't know the words, the grammar, the syntax. And—"

Something else was happening in her Oriental face, and he strained to catch it. "Yes?"

"—Babel-17."

"The language?"

"Yes. You know what I used to call my 'knack'?"

"You mean you suddenly understood the language?"

"Well, General Forester had just told me what I had was not a monologue, but a dialogue, which I hadn't known before. That fitted in with some other things I had in the back of my mind. I realized I could tell where the voices changed myself. And then——"

"Do you understand it?"

"I understand some of it better than I did this afternoon. There's something about the language itself that scares me even more than General Forester."

Puzzlement fixed itself to T'mwarba's face. "About the language itself?"

She nodded.

"What?"

The muscle in her cheek jumped again. "For one thing, I think I know where the next accident is going to be."

"Accident?"

"Yes. The next sabotage that the Invaders are planning, if it is the Invaders, which I'm not sure of. But the language itself—it's . . . it's strange."

"How?"

"Small," she said. "Tight. Close together— That doesn't mean anything to you, does it? In a language, I mean?"

"Compactness?" asked Dr. T'mwarba. "I would think it's a good quality in a spoken language."

"Yes," and the sibilant became a breath. "Mocky, I am scared!"

"Why?"

"Because I'm going to try to do something, and I don't know if I can or not."

"If it's worth trying, you should be a little afraid. What is it?"

"I decided it back in the bar, and I figured out I'd better talk to somebody first. That usually means you."

"Give."

"I'm going to solve this whole Babel-17 business myself."

T'mwarba leaned his head to the right.

"Because I have to find out who speaks this language, where it comes from, and what it's trying to say."

His head went left.

"Why? Well, most textbooks say language is a mechanism for expressing thought, Mocky. But language *is* thought. Thought is information given form. The form is language. The form of this language is . . . amazing."

"What amazes you?"

"Mocky, when you learn another tongue, you learn the way another people see the world, the universe."

He nodded.

"And as I see into this language, I begin to see . . . too much."

"It sounds very poetical."

She laughed. "You always say that to me to bring me back to earth."

"Which I don't have to do too often. Good poets tend to be practical and abhor mysticism."

"Something about trying to hit reality; you figure it out," she said. "Only, as poetry tries to touch something real, maybe this is poetical."

"All right. I still don't understand. But how do you propose to solve the Babel-17 mystery?"

"You really want to know?" Her hands fell to her knees. "I'm going to get a spaceship, get a crew together, and get to the scene of the next accident."

"That's right, you do have Interstellar Captain's papers. Can you afford it?"

"The government's going to subsidize it."

"Oh, fine. But why?"

"I'm familiar with a half-dozen languages of the Invaders. Babel-17 isn't one of them. It isn't a language of the Alliance. I want to find out who speaks this language— because I want to find out who, or what, in the Universe thinks that way. Do you think I can, Mocky?"

"Have another cup of coffee." He reached back over his shoulder and sailed the carafe across to her again. "That's a good question. There's a lot to consider. You're not the most stable person in the world. Managing a spaceship crew takes a special sort of psychology which—you have. Your papers,

if I remember, were the result of that odd—eh, marriage of
yours, a couple of years ago. But you only used an automatic
crew. For a trip this length, won't you be managing Transport
people?"

She nodded.

"Most of my dealings have been with Customs persons.
You're more or less Customs."

"Both parents were Transport. I was Transport up till the
time of the Embargo."

"That's true. Suppose I say, 'yes, I think you can'?"

"I'd say, 'thanks,' and leave tomorrow."

"Suppose I said I'd like a week to check over your
psyche-indices with a microscope, while you took a vacation
at my place, taught no classes, gave no public readings,
avoided cocktail parties?"

"I'd say, 'thanks'. And leave tomorrow."

He grinned. "Then why are you bothering me?"

"Because——" She shrugged. "Because tomorrow I'm
going to be busy as the devil . . . and I won't have time to say
good-bye."

"Oh." The wryness of his grin relaxed into a smile.

And he thought about the myna bird again.

Rydra, thin, thirteen, and gawky, had broken through the
triple doors of the conservatory with the new thing called
laughter she had just discovered how to make in her mouth.
And he was parental proud that the near corpse, who had
been given into his charge six months ago, was now a girl
again, with boy-cropped hair and sulks and tantrums and
questions and caresses for the two guinea pigs she had named
Lump and Lumpkin. The air-conditioning pressed back the
shrubbery to the glass wall and sun struck through the
transparent roof. She had said, "What's that, Mocky?"

And he, smiling at her, sun-spotted in white shorts and
superfluous halter, said, "It's a myna bird. It'll talk to you.
Say hello."

The black eye was dead as a raisin with a pinhead of live
light jammed in the corner. The feathers glistened and the
needle beak lazed over a thick tongue. She cocked her head
as the bird head cocked, and whispered, "Hello?"

Dr. T"mwarba had trained it for two weeks with freshdug earthworms to surprise her. The bird looked over its left shoulder and droned, *"Hello, Rydra, it's a fine day out and I'm happy."*

Screaming.

As unexpected as that.

He'd thought she'd started to laugh. But her face was contorted, she began to beat at something with her arms, stagger backwards, fall. The scream rasped in near collapsed lungs, choked, rasped again. He ran to gather up her flailing, hysterical figure, while the drone of the bird's voice undercut her wailing: *"It's a fine day out and I'm happy."*

He'd seen acute anxiety attacks before. But this shook him. When she could talk about it later, she simply said— tensely, with white lips, "It frightened me!"

Which would have been it, had the damn bird not gotten loose three days later and flown up into the antenna net he and Rydra had put up together for her amateur radio stasis-crafter with which she could listen to the hyperstatic communications of the transport ships in this arm of the galaxy. A wing and a leg got caught, and it began to beat against one of the hot lines so that you could see the sparks even in the sunlight. "We've got to get him out of there!" Rydra had cried. Her fingertips were over her mouth, but as she looked at the bird, he could see the color draining from under her tan. "I'll take care of it, honey," he said. "You just forget about him."

"If he hits that wire a couple of more times he'll be dead!"

But he had already started inside for the ladder. When he came out, he stopped. She had shinnied four-fifths up the guy wire on the leaning catalpa tree that shaded the corner of the house. Fifteen seconds later he was watching her reach out, draw back, reach out again toward the wild feathers. He knew damn well she wasn't afraid of the hot line, either; she'd strung it up herself. Sparks again. So she made up her mind and grabbed. A minute later she was coming across the yard, holding the rumpled bird at arm's length. Her face looked as if it had been blown across with powdered lime.

"Take it, Mocky," she said, with no voice behind her trembling lips, "before it says something and I start hollering again."

So now, thirteen years later, something else was speaking to her, and she said she was scared. He knew how scared she could be; he also knew with what bravery she could face down her fears.

He said, "Good-bye. I'm glad you woke me up. I'd be mad as a damp rooster if you hadn't come. Thank you."

"The thanks is yours, Mocky," she said. "I'm still frightened."

III

Daniel D. Appleby, who seldom thought of himself by his name—he was a Customs Officer—stared at the order through wire-framed glasses and rubbed his hand across his crew-cut red hair. "Well, it says you can, if you want to."

"And——?"

"And it is signed by General Forester."

"Then I expect you to cooperate."

"But I have to approve——"

"Then you'll come along and approve on the spot. I don't have time to send the reports in and wait for processing."

"But there's no way——"

"Yes, there is. Come with me."

"But Miss Wong, I don't walk around Transport town at night."

"I enjoy it. Scared?"

"Not exactly. But——"

"I have to get a ship and a crew by the morning. And it's General Forester's signature. All right?"

"I suppose so."

"Then come on. I have to get my crew approved."

Insistent and protesting respectively, Rydra and the officer left the bronze and glass building.

They waited for the monorail nearly six minutes. When

they came down, the streets were smaller, and a continuous whine of transport ships fell across the sky. Warehouses and repair and supply shops sandwiched rickety apartments and rooming houses. A larger street cut past, rumbling with traffic, busy loaders, stellarmen. They passed neon entertainments, restaurants of many worlds, bars, and brothels. In the crush the Customs Officer pulled his shoulders in, walked more quickly to keep up with Rydra's long-legged stride.

"Where do you intend to find—?"

"My pilot? That's who I want to pick up first." She stopped on the corner, shoved her hands into the pockets of her leather pants, and looked around.

"Do you have someone in mind?"

"I'm thinking of several people. This way." They turned on a narrower street, more cluttered, more brightly lit.

"Where are we going? Do you know this section?"

But she laughed, slipped her arm through his, and, like a dancer leading without pressure, she turned him toward an iron stairway.

"In here?"

"Have you ever been to this place before?" she asked with an innocent eagerness that made him feel for a moment he was escorting her.

He shook his head.

Up from the basement cafe black burst—a man, ebony-skinned, with red and green jewels set into his chest, face, arms, and thighs. Moist membranes, also jeweled, fell from his arms, billowing on slender tines as he hurried up the steps.

Rydra caught his shoulder. "Hey, Lome!"

"Captain Wong!" The voice was high, the white teeth needle-filed. He whirled to her with extending sails. Pointed ears shifted forward. "What you here for?"

"Lome, Brass is wrestling tonight?"

"You want to see him? Aye, Skipper, with the Silver Dragon, and it's an even match. Hey, I look for you on Deneb. I buy your book too. Can't read much, but I buy. And I no find you. Where you been a' six months?"

"Earthside, teaching at the University. But I'm going out again."

"You ask Brass for pilot? You heading out Specelli way?"

"That's right."

Lome dropped his black arm around her shoulder and the sail cloaked her, shimmering. "You go out Caesar, you call Lome for pilot, ever you do. Know Caesar———" He screwed his face and shook his head. "Nobody know it better."

"When I do, I will. But now it's Specelli."

"Then you do good with Brass. Work with him before?"

"We got drunk together when we were both quarantined for a week on one of the Cygnet planetoids. He seemed to know what he was talking about."

"Talk, talk, talk," Lome derided. "Yeah, I remember you, Captain who talk. You go watch that son of a dog wrestle; then you know what sort of pilot he make."

"That's what I came to do." Rydra turned to the Customs Officer, who shrank against the iron banister. (God, he thought, she's going to introduce me!) But she cocked her head with a half smile and turned back. "I'll see you again, Lome, when I get home."

"Yeah, yeah, you say that and say that twice. But I no in six months see you." He laughed. "But I like you, lady Captain. Take me to Caesar some day, I show you."

"When I go, you go, Lome."

A needle leer. "Go, go, you say. I got go now. Bye-bye, lady Captain"—he bowed and touched his head in salute— "Captain Wong." And was gone.

"You shouldn't be afraid of him," Rydra told the Officer,

"But he's———" During his search for a word, he wondered, How did she know? "Where in five hells did he come from?"

"He's an Earthman. Though I believe he was born en route from Arcturus to one of the Centauris. His mother was a Slug, I think, if he wasn't lying about that too. Lome tells tall tales."

"You mean all that getup is cosmetisurgery?"

"Um-hm." Rydra started down the stairs.

"But why the devil do they do that to themselves?

They're all so weird. That's why decent people won't have anything to do with them."

"Sailors used to get tattoos. Besides, Lome has nothing else to do. I doubt he's had a pilot's job in forty years."

"He's not a good pilot? What was all that about the Caesar nebula?"

"I'm sure he knows it. But he's at least a hundred and twenty years old. After eighty, your reflexes start to go, and that's the end of a pilot's career. He just shuttle-bums from port city to port city, knows everything that happens to everybody, stays good for gossip and advice."

They entered the cafe on a ramp that swerved above the heads of the customers drinking at bar and table thirty feet below. Above and to the side of them, a fifty-foot sphere hovered like smoke, under spotlights, Rydra looked from the globe to the Customs Officer. "They haven't started the games yet."

"Is this where they hold those *fights?*"

"That's right."

"But that's supposed to be illegal!"

"Never passed the bill. After they debated, it got shelved."

"Oh."

As they descended among the jovial transport workers, the Officer blinked. Most were ordinary men and women, but the results of cosmetisurgery were numerous enough to keep his eyes leaping. "I've never *been* in a place like this before!" he whispered. Amphibian or reptilian creatures argued and laughed with griffins and metallic-skinned sphinxes.

"Leave your clothing here?" smiled the check girl. Her naked skin was candy green, her immense coif piled like pink cotton. Her breasts, navel, and lips flashed.

"I don't believe so," the Customs Officer said quickly.

"At least take your shoes and shirt off," Rydra said, slipping off her blouse. "People will think you're strange." She bent, rose and handed her sandals over the counter. She had begun to unbuckle her waist cinch when she caught his desperate look, smiled, and fastened the buckle again.

Carefully he removed jacket, vest, shirt, and undershirt. He was about to untie his shoes when someone grabbed his arm. "Hey Customs!"

He stood up before a huge, naked man with a frown on his pocked face like a burst in rotten rind. His only ornaments were mechanical beetle lights that swarmed in patterns over his chest, shoulders, legs, and arms.

"Eh, pardon me?"

"What you doing here, Customs?"

"Sir, I am not bothering you."

"And I'm not bothering you. Have a drink, Customs. I'm being friendly."

"Thank you very much, but I'd rather——"

"I'm being friendly. You're not. If you're not gonna be friendly, Customs, I'm not gonna be friendly either."

"Well, I'm with some——" He looked helplessly at Rydra.

"Come on. Then you both have a drink. On me. Real friendly, damn it." His other hand fell toward Rydra's shoulder, but she caught his wrist. The fingers opened from the many scaled stellarimeter grafted onto his palm. "Navigator?"

He nodded, and she let the hand go, which landed.

"Why *are* you so 'friendly' tonight?"

The intoxicated man shook his head. His hair was knotted in a stubby black braid over his left ear. "I'm just friendly with Customs here. I like you."

"Thanks. Buy us that drink and I'll buy you one back."

As he nodded heavily, his green eyes narrowed. He reached between her breasts and fingered up the gold disk that hung from the chain around her neck. "*Captain* Wong?"

She nodded.

"Better not mess with you, then." He laughed. "Come on, Captain, and I'll buy you and Customs here something to make you happy." They pushed their way to the bar.

What was green and came in small glasses at more respectable establishments, here was served in mugs.

"Who you betting on in the Dragon/Brass skirmish, and if you say the Dragon, I'll throw this in your face. Joking, of course, Captain."

"I'm not betting," Rydra said. "I'm hiring. You know Brass?"

"Was a navigator on his last trip. Got in a week ago."

"You're friendly for the same reason he's wrestling?"

"You might say that."

The Customs Officer scratched his collarbone and looked puzzled.

"Last trip Brass made went bust," Rydra explained to him. "The crew is out of work. Brass is on exhibit tonight." She turned again to the Navigator. "Will there be many captains bidding for him?"

He put his tongue under his upper lip, squinted one eye and dropped his head. He shrugged.

"I'm the only one you've run into?"

A nod, a large swallow of liquor.

"What's your name?"

"Calli, Navigator-Two."

"Where are your One and Three?"

"Three's over there somewhere getting drunk. One was a sweet girl named Cathy O'Higgin's. She's dead." He finished the drink and reached over for another one.

"My treat," Rydra said. "Why's she dead?"

"Ran into Invaders. Only people who ain't dead, Brass, me, and Three, and our Eye. Lost the whole platoon, our Slug. Damn good Slug too. Captain, that was a bad trip. The Eye, he cracked up without the Ear and Nose. They'd been discorporate for ten years together. Ron, Cathy, and me, we'd only been tripled for a couple of months. But even so . . ." He shook his head. "It's bad."

"Call your Three over," Rydra said.

"Why?"

"I'm looking for a full crew."

Calli wrinkled his forehead. "We don't got no One anymore."

"You're going to mope around here forever? Go to the Morgue."

Calli *humphed*. "You wanna see my Three, you come on."

Rydra shrugged in aquiescence, and the Customs Officer followed behind them.

"Hey, stupid, swing around."

The kid who turned on the bar stool was maybe nineteen. The Customs Officer thought of a snarl of metal bands. Calli was a large, comfortable man—

"Captain Wong, this is Ron, best Three to come out of the Solar System."

—but Ron was small, thin, with uncannily sharp muscular definition: pectorals like scored metal plates beneath drawn wax skin; stomach like ridged hosing, arms like braided cables. Even the facial muscles stood at the back of the jaw and jammed against the separate columns of his neck. He was unkempt and towheaded and sapphire eyed, but the only cosmetisurgery evident was the bright rose growing on his shoulder. He flung out a quick smile and touched his forehead with a forefinger in salute. His nails were nub-gnawed on fingers like knotted lengths of white rope.

"Captain Wong is looking for a crew."

Ron shifted on the stool, raising his head a little; every other muscle in his body moved too, like snakes under milk.

The Customs Officer saw Rydra's eyes widen. Not understanding her reaction, he ignored it.

"Don't got no One," Ron said. His smile was quick and sad again.

"Suppose I found a One for you?"

The Navigators looked at each other.

Calli turned to Rydra and rubbed the side of his nose with his thumb. "You know the thing about a triple like us——"

Rydra's left hand caught her right. "Like this, you have to be. My choice is subject to your approval, of course."

"Well, it's pretty difficult for someone else——"

"It's impossible. But it's your choice. I just make suggestions. But my suggestions are damn good ones. What do you say?"

Calli's thumb moved from his nose to his earlobe. He shrugged. "You can't make an offer much better than that."

Rydra looked at Ron.

The kid put one foot up on the stool, hugged his knee, and peered across his patella. "I say, let's see who you suggest."

She nodded. "Fair."

"You know, jobs for broken triples aren't that easy to come by." Calli put his hand on Ron's shoulder.

"Yeah, but——"

Rydra looked up. "Let's watch the wrestling."

Along the counter people raised their heads. At the tables, patrons released the catch in their chair arms so that the backs swung to half recline.

Calli's mug clinked on the counter, and Ron raised both feet to the stool and leaned back against the bar.

"What are they looking at?" the Customs Officer asked. "Where's everybody———" Rydra put her hand on the back of his neck and did something so that he laughed and swung his head up. Then he sucked a great breath and let it out slowly.

The smoky, null-grav globe, hung in the vault, was shot with colored light. The room had gone dim. Thousands of watts of floodlights struck the plastic surface and gleamed on the faces below as smoke in the bright sphere faded.

"What's going to happen?" the Customs Officer asked. "Is that where they wrestle . . . ?"

Rydra brushed her hand over his mouth and he nearly swallowed his tongue: but was quiet.

And the Silver Dragon came, wings working in the smoke, silver feathers like clashed blades, scales on the grand haunches shaking; she rippled her ten-foot body and squirmed in the antigravity field, green lips leering, silver lids batting over green. "It's a woman!" breathed the Customs Officer.

An appreciative tattoo of finger snapping scattered through the audience.

Smoke rolled in the globe—

"That's our Brass!" whispered Calli.

—and Brass yawned and shook his head, ivory saber teeth glistening with spittle, muscles humped on shoulders and arms; brass claws unsheathed six inches from yellow plush paws. Bunched bands on his belly bent above them. The barbed tail beat on the globe's wall. His mane, sheared to prevent handholds, ran like water.

Calli grabbed the Customs Officer's shoulder. "Snap your fingers, man! That's *our* Brass!"

The Customs Officer, who had never been able to, nearly broke his hand trying.

The globe flared red. The two pilots turned to one another across the sphere's diameter. Voices quieted. The

Customs Officer glanced from the ceiling to the people around him. Every other face was up. The Navigator, Three, was hunched in a foetal knot on the bar stool. Copper shifting; Rydra too dropped her eyes to glance at the lean bunched arms and straited thighs of the rose-shouldered boy.

Above, the opponents flexed and stretched, drifting. A sudden movement from the Dragon, and Brass drew back, then launched from the wall.

. The Customs Officer grabbed something.

The two forms struck, grappled, spun against a wall and ricocheted. People began to stamp. Arm reached over arm, leg wrapped around leg, till Brass whirled loose from her and was hurled to the upper wall of the arena. Shaking his head, he righted. Below, alert, the Dragon twisted and writhed, anticipation jerked her wings. Brass leapt from the ceiling, reversed suddenly, and caught the Dragon with his hind feet. She staggered back, flailing. Saber teeth came together and missed.

"What are they trying to do?" the Customs Officer whispered. "How can you tell who's winning?" He looked down again: what he'd grabbed was Calli's shoulder.

"When one can throw the other against the wall and only touch the far wall himself with one limb on the ricochet," Calli explained, not looking down, "that's a fall."

The Silver Dragon snapped her body like bent metal released, and Brass shot away and spread-eagled against the globe. But as she floated back to take the shock on one hind leg, she lost her balance and the second leg touched, too.

An anticipatory breath loosed in the audience. Encouraging snapping; Brass recovered, leaped, pushed her to the wall, but his rebound was too sharp and he, too, staggered on three limbs.

A twist in the center again. The Dragon snarled, stretched, shook her scales. Brass glowered, peered with eyes like gold coins hooded, spun back quaking, then leapt forward.

Silver whirled beneath his shoulder blow, hit the globe. She looked for the world as if she were trying to climb the wall. Brass rebounded lightly, caught himself on one paw, then pushed away.

The globe flashed green, and Calli pounded the bar. "Look at him show that tinsel bitch!"

Grappling limbs braided one another, and claw caught claw till the stifled arms shook, broke apart. Two more falls that went to neither side; then the Silver Dragon came head first into Brass' chest, knocked him back, and recovered on tail alone. Below the crowd stamped.

"That's a foul!" Calli exclaimed, shaking the Customs Officer away. "Damn it, that's a foul!" But the globe flashed green again. Officially the second fall was hers.

Warily now they swam in the sphere. Twice the Dragon feinted, and Brass jerked aside his claws or sucked in his belly to avoid hers.

"Why don't she lay off him?" Calli demanded of the sky. "She's nagging him to death. Grapple and fight!"

As if in answer, Brass sprang, swiping her shoulder; what would have been a perfect fall got messed up because the Dragon caught his arm and he swerved off, smashing clumsily against the plastic.

"She can't do that!" This time it was the Customs Officer. He grabbed Calli again. "Can she do that? I don't think they should allow——" And he bit his tongue because Brass swung back, hauled her from the wall, flipped her between his legs, and as she scrambled off the plastic, he bounced on his forearm and hovered centrally, flexing for the crowd.

"That's it!" cried Calli. "Two out of three!"

The globe flashed green again. Snapping broke into applause. "Did he win?" demanded the Customs Officer. "Did he win?"

"Listen! Of course he won! Hey, let's go see him. Come on, Captain!"

Rydra had already started through the crowd. Ron sprang behind her, and Calli, dragging the Customs Officer, came after. A flight of black tile steps took them into a room with couches where a few groups of men and women stood around Condor, a great gold and crimson creature, who was being made ready to fight Ebony who waited alone in the corner. The arena exit opened and Brass came in sweating.

"Hey," Calli called. "Hey, that was great, boy. And the Captain here wants to talk to you."

Brass stretched, then dropped to all fours, a low rumble
in his chest. He shook his mane, then his gold eyes widened
in recognition. "Ca'tain Wong!" The mouth, distended through
cosmetisurgically implanted fangs, could not deal with a
plosive labial unless it was voiced. "How you'd like me
tonight?"

"Well enough to want you to pilot me through the
Specelli." She roughed a tuft of yellow behind his ear. "You
said sometime ago you'd like to show me what you could
do."

"Yeah," Brass nodded. "I just think I'm dreaming." He
pulled away his loin rag and swabbed his neck and arms with
the bunched cloth, then caught the Customs Officer's amazed
expression. "Just cosmetisurgery." He kept on swabbing.

"Hand him your psyche-rating," Rydra said, "and he'll
approve you."

"That means we leave tomorrow, Ca'tain?"

"At dawn."

From his belt pouch Brass drew a thin metal card. "Here
you go, Customs."

The Customs Officer scanned the runic marking. On a
metal tracing plate from his back pocket, he noted the shift in
stability index, but decided to integrate for the exact summation later on. Practice told him it was well above acceptable.
"Miss Wong, I mean Captain Wong, what about their cards?"
He turned to Calli and Ron.

Ron reached behind his neck and rubbed his scapula.
"You don't worry about us till you get a Navigator-One."
The hard, adolescent face held an engaging belligerence.

"We'll check them later," Rydra said. "We've got more
people to find first."

"You're looking for a full crew?" asked Brass.

Rydra nodded. "What about the Eye that came back
with you?"

Brass shook his head. "Lost his Ear and Nose. They
were a real close tri'le, Ca'tain. He hung around maybe six
hours before he went back to the Morgue."

"I see. Can you recommend anyone?"

"No one in 'articular. Just hang around the Discor'orate
Sector and see what turns u'."

"If you want a crew by morning, we better start now," said Calli.

"Let's go," said Rydra.

As they walked to the ramp's foot, the Customs Officer asked. "The Discorporate Sector?"

"What about it?" Rydra was at the rear of the group.

"That's so—well, I don't like the idea."

Rydra laughed. "Because of the dead men? They won't hurt you."

"And I know *that's* illegal, for bodily persons to be in the Discorporate Sector."

"In certain parts," Rydra corrected, and the other men laughed now. "We'll stay out of the illegal sections—if we can."

"Would you like your clothes back?" the check-girl asked.

People had been stopping to congratulate Brass, pounding at his hip with appreciative fists and snapping their fingers. Now he swung his contour cape over his head. It fell to his shoulders, clasped his neck, draped under his arms and around his thick hams. Brass waved to the crowd and started up the ramp.

"You can really judge a pilot by watching him wrestle?" the officer inquired of Rydra.

She nodded. "In the ship, the pilot's nervous system is connected directly with the controls. The whole hyperstasis transit consists of him literally wrestling the stasis shifts. You judge by his reflexes, his ability to control his artificial body. An experienced Transporter can tell exactly how he'll work with hyperstasis currents."

"I'd heard about it, of course. But this was the first time I've seen it. I mean in person. It was . . . exciting."

"Yes," Rydra said, "isn't it?"

As they reached the ramp's head, lights again pierced the globe. Ebony and Condor circled in the fighting sphere.

On the sidewalk Brass dropped back, loping on all fours, to Rydra's side. "What about a Slug and a 'latoon?"

The platoon was a group of twelve who did all the mechanical jobs on the ship. Such simple work was done by the very young, so they usually needed a nursemaid: that was the Slug.

"I'd like to get a one-trip platoon if I can."

"Why so green?"

"I want to train them my way. The older groups tend to be too set."

"A one-tri' grou' can be a hell of a 'roblem to disci'line. And inefficient as 'iss, so I've heard. Never been with one myself."

"As long as there're no out and out nuts, I don't care. Besides, if I want one now, I can be surer of getting one by morning if I put my order in at Navy."

Brass nodded. "Your request in yet?"

"I want to check with my pilot first and see if you had any preferences."

They were passing a street phone on the corner lamp-post. Rydra ducked beneath the plastic hood. A minute later she was saying, "—a platoon for a run toward Specelli scheduled at dawn tomorrow. I know that it's short notice, but I don't need a particularly seasoned group. Even a one trip will do." She looked from under the hood and winked at them. "Fine. I'll call later to get their psyche-indices for Customs approval. Yes, I have an Officer with me. Thank you."

She came from under the hood. "Closest way to the Discorporate Sector is through there."

The streets narrowed about them, twisting through one another, deserted. Then a stretch of concrete where metal turrets rose. Crossed, and recrossed, wires webbed them. Pylons of bluish light dropped half shadows.

"Is this . . . ?" the Customs Officer began. Then he was quiet. Walking out, they slowed their steps. Against the darkness red light shot between towers.

"What . . . ?"

"Just a transfer. They go on all night," Calli explained. Green lightning crackled to their left.

"Transfer?"

"It's a quick exchange of energies resulting from the relocation of discorporate states," the Navigator-Two volunteered glibly.

"But I still don't . . ."

They had moved between the pylons now when a flickering coalesced. Silver latticed with red fire glimmered through industrial smog. Three figures formed: the women's sequined skeletons glittered toward them, casting hollow eyes.

Kittens clawed the Customs Officer's back, for strut work pylons gleamed behind the apparitional bellies.

"The faces," he whispered. "As soon as you look away, you can't remember what they look like. When you look at them, they look like people, but when you look away——" He caught his breath as another passed. "You can't remember!" He stared after them. "Dead?" He shook his head. "You know I've been approving psyche-indices on Transport workers corporate and discorporate for ten years. And I've never been close enough to speak to a discorporate soul. Oh, I've seen pictures and occasionally passed one of the less fantastic on the street. But this . . ."

"There're some jobs"—Calli's voice was as heavy with alcohol as his shoulders with muscle—"some jobs on a Transport Ship you just can't give to a live human being."

"I know, I know," said the Customs Officer. "So you use dead ones."

"That's right." Calli nodded. "Like the Eye, Ear, and Nose. A live human scanning all that goes on in those hyperstasis frequencies would—well, die first, and go crazy second."

"I do know the theory," the Customs Officer stated sharply.

Calli suddenly cupped the Officer's cheek in his hand and pulled him close to his own pocked face. "You don't know anything, Customs." The tone was of their first exchange in the cafe. "Aw, you hide in your Customs cage, cage hid in the safe gravity of Earth, Earth held firm by the sun, sun fixed headlong toward Vega, all in the predicted tide of this spiral arm——" He gestured across night where the Milky Way would run over a less bright city. "And you never break free!" Suddenly he pushed the little spectacled red head away. "Ehhh! You have nothing to say to me!"

The bereaved navigator caught a guy cable slanting from support to concrete. It *twanged*. The low note set something loose in the Officer's throat which reached his mouth with the metal taste of outrage.

He would have spat it, but Rydra's copper eyes were now as close to his face as the hostile, pitted visage had been.

She said: "He was part," the words lean, calm, her eyes intent on not losing his, "of a triple, a close, precarious, emotional, and sexual relation with two other people. And one of them has just died."

The edge of her tone hued away the bulk of the Officer's anger; but a sliver escaped him: "Perverts!"

Ron put his head to the side, his musculature showing clear the double of hurt and bewilderment. "There're some jobs," he echoed Calli's syntax, "some jobs on a Transport Ship you just can't give to two people alone. The jobs are too complicated."

"I *know*." Then he thought, I've hurt the boy, too. Calli leaned on a girder. Something else was working in the Officer's mouth.

"*You* have something to say," Rydra said.

Surprise that she knew prized his lips. He looked from Calli to Ron, back. "I'm sorry for you."

Calli's brows raised, then returned, his expression settling. "I'm sorry for you too."

Brass reared. "There's a transfer conclave about a quarter of a mile down in the medium energy states. That would attract the sort of Eye, Ear, and Nose you want for Specelli." He grinned at the Officer through his fangs. "That's one of your illegal sections. The hallucination count goes way u', and some cor'orate egos can't handle it. But most sane 'eo'le don't have any 'roblem."

"If it's illegal, I'd just as soon wait here," the Customs Officer said. "You can just come back and pick me up. I'll approve their indices then."

Rydra nodded. Calli threw one arm around the waist of the ten-foot pilot, the other around Ron's shoulder. "Come on, Captain, if you want to get your crew by morning."

"If we don't find what we want in an hour, we'll be back anyway," she said.

The Customs Officer watched them move away between the slim towers.

IV

—recall from broken banks and color of earth breaking
into clear pool water her eyes; the figure blinking her eyes
and speaking.

He said: "An Officer, ma'am. A Customs Officer."

Surprise at her witty return, at first hurt, then amusement
following. He answered: "About ten years. How long have
you been discorporate?"

And she moved closer to him, her hair holding the
recalled odor of. And the sharp transparent features reminding
him of. More words from her, now, making him laugh.

"Yes, this is all very new to me. Doesn't the whole
vagueness with which everything seems to happen get you,
too?"

Again her answer, both coaxing and witty.

"Well, yes," he smiled. "For you I guess it wouldn't
be."

Her ease infected him; and either she reached playfully
to take his hand or he amazed himself by taking hers, and the
apparition was real beneath his fingers with skin as smooth
as.

"You're so forward. I mean I'm not used to young
women just coming up and . . . behaving like this."

Her charming logic again explained it away, making him
feel her near, nearer, nearing, and her banter made music, a
phrase from.

"Well, yes, you're discorporate, so it doesn't matter.
But——"

And her interruption was a word or a kiss or a frown or a smile, sending not humor through him now, but luminous amazement, fear, excitement; and the feel of her shape against his completely new. He fought to retain it, pattern of pressure and pressure, fading as the pressure itself faded. She was going away. She was laughing like, as though, as if. He stood, losing her laughter, replaced by whirled bewilderment in the tides of his consciousness fading—

V

When they returned, Brass called, "Good news! We got who we wanted."

"Crew's coming along," commented Calli.

Rydra handed him the three index cards. "They'll report to the ship discorporate two hours before—what's wrong?"

Danil D. Appleby reached to take the cards. "I . . . she . . ." and couldn't say anything else.

"Who?" Rydra asked. The concern on her face was driving away even his remaining memories, and he resented it, memories of, of.

Calli laughed. "A succubus! While we were gone, he got hustled by a succubus!"

"Yeah!" from Brass. "Look at him!" Ron laughed, too.

"It was a woman . . . I think. I can remember what *I* said——"

"How much did she take you for?" Brass asked.

"Take me?"

Ron said, "I don't think he knows."

Calli grinned at the Navigator-Three and then at the Officer. "Take a look in your billfold."

"Huh?"

"Take a look."

Incredulously he reached in his pocket. The metallic envelope flipped apart in his hands. "Ten . . . twenty . . . But I had *fifty* in here when I left the cafe!"

Calli slapped his thighs laughing. He loped over and encircled the Customs Officer's shoulder. "You'll end up a Transport man after that happens a couple of more times."

"But she . . . I . . ." The emptiness of his thefted recollections was real as any love loss. The rifled wallet seemed trivial. Tears banked his eyes. "But she was——" Confusion snarled the sentence's end.

"What was she, friend?" Calli asked.

"She . . . was." That was the sad entirety.

"Since discor'oration, you *can* take it with you," said Brass. "They try for it with some 'retty shady methods, too. I'd be embarrassed to tell you how many times that's ha''ened to me."

"She left you enough to get home with," Rydra said. "I'll reimburse you."

"No, I . . ."

"Come on, Captain. He paid for it, and he got his money's worth, aye, Customs?"

Choking on the embarrassment, he nodded.

"Then . . . check these ratings," Rydra said. "We still have a Slug to pick up, and a Navigator-One."

At a public phone, Rydra called back to Navy. Yes, a platoon had turned up. A Slug had been recommended along with them. "Fine," Rydra said, and handed the phone to the officer. He took the psyche-indices from the clerk and incorporated them for final integration with the Eye, Ear, and Nose cards that Rydra had given him. The Slug looked particularly favorable. "Seems to be a talented coordinator," he ventured.

"Can't have too good a Slug. Es'ecially with a new 'latoon." Brass shook his mane. "He's got to keep those kids in line."

"This one should do it. Highest compatibility index I've seen in a long while."

"What's the hostility on him?" asked Calli. "Compatibility, hell! Can he give your butt a good kick when you need it?"

The Officer shrugged. "He weighs two hundred and seventy pounds and he's only five nine. Have you met a fat person yet who wasn't mean as a rat underneath it all?"

"There you go!" Calli laughed.

"Where do we go to fix the wound?" Brass asked Rydra.

She raised her brows questioningly.

"To get a first navigator," he explained.

"To the Morgue."

Ron frowned. Calli looked puzzled. The flashing bugs collared his neck, then spilled his chest, scattering. "You know our first navigator's got to be a girl who will——"

"She will be," Rydra said.

They left the Discorporate Sector and took the monorail through the tortuous remains of Transport Town, then along the edge of the space-field. Blackness beyond the windows was flung with blue signal lights. Ships rose with a white flare, blued through distance, became bloody stars in the rusted air.

They joked for the first twenty minutes over the humming runners. The fluorescent ceiling dropped greenish light on their faces, in their laps. One by one, the Customs Officer watched them go silent while the side-to-side inertia became a headlong drive. He had not spoken at all, still trying to regain her face, her words, her shape. But it stayed away, frustrating as the imperative comment that leaves your mind as speech begins, and the mouth is left empty, a lost referent to love.

When they stepped onto the open platform at Thule Station, warm wind flushed the east. The clouds had shattered under an ivory moon. Gravel and granite silvered the broken edges. Behind was the city's red mist. Before, on broken night, rose the black Morgue.

They went down the steps and walked quietly through the stone park. The garden of water and rock was eerie. Nothing grew here.

At the door slabbed metal without external light blotted the darkness. "How do you get in?" the Officer asked, as they climbed the shallow steps.

Rydra lifted the Captain's pendant from her neck and

placed it against a small disk. Something hummed, and light divided the entrance as the doors slid back. Rydra stepped through, the rest followed.

Calli stared at the metallic vaults overhead. "You know there's enough transport meat deep-frozen in this place to service a hundred stars and all their planets."

"And Customs people too," said the Officer.

"Does anybody ever bother to call back a Customs who decided to take a rest?" Ron asked with candid ingenuousness.

"Don't know what for," said Calli.

"It's been known to happen," responded the Officer dryly. "Occasionally."

"More rarely than with Transport," Rydra said. "As of yet, the Customs work involved in getting ships from star to star is a science. The transport work maneuvering through hyperstasis levels is still an art. In a hundred years they may both be sciences. Fine. But today a person who learns the rules of art well is a little rarer than the person who learns the rules of science. Also, there's a tradition involved. Transport people are used to dying and getting called back, working with dead men or live. This is still a little hard for Customs to take. Over here to the Suicides."

They left the main lobby for the labeled corridor that sloped up through the storage chamber. It emptied them onto a platform in an indirectly lighted room, racked up its hundred-foot height with glass cases, catwalked and laddered like a spider's den. In the coffins, dark shapes were rigid beneath frost shot glass.

"What I don't understand about this whole business," the Officer whispered, "is the calling back. Can anybody who dies be made corporate again? You're right, Captain Wong, in Customs it's almost impolite to talk about things like . . . this."

"Any suicide who discorporates through regular Morgue channels can be called back. But a violent death where the Morgue just retrieves the body afterward, or the run of the mill senile ending that most of us hit at a hundred and fifty or so, then you're dead forever; although there, if you pass through regular channels, your brain pattern is recorded and your thinking ability can be tapped if anyone wants it, though your consciousness is gone wherever consciousness goes."

Beside them, a twelve-foot filing crystal glowed like pink quartz. "Ron," said Rydra. "No, Ron and Calli too."

The Navigators stepped up, puzzled.

"You know some first navigator who suicided recently that you think we might——"

Rydra shook her head. She passed her hand before the filing crystal. In the concaved screen at the base, words flashed. She stilled her fingers. "Navigator-Two. . . ." She turned her hand. "Navigator-One. . . ." She paused and ran her hand in a different direction. ". . . male, male, male, female. Now, you talk to me, Calli, Ron."

"Huh? About what?" .

"About yourselves, about what you want."

Rydra's eyes moved back and forth between the screen and the man and boy beside her.

"Well, huh . . . ?" Calli scratched his head.

"Pretty," said Ron. "I want her to be pretty." He leaned forward, an intense light in his blue eyes.

"Oh, yes," said Calli, "but she can't be a sweet, plump Irish girl with black hair and agate eyes and freckles that come out after four days of sun. She can't have the slightest lisp that makes you tingle even when she reels off her calculations quicker and more accurate than a computer voice, yet still lisping, or makes you tingle when she holds your head in her lap and tells you about how much she needs to feel——"

"Calli!" from Ron.

And the big man stopped with his fist against his stomach, breathing hard.

Rydra watched, her hand drifting through centimeters over the crystal's face. The names on the screen flashed back and forth.

"But pretty," Ron repeated. "And likes sports, to wrestle, I think, when we're planet side. Cathy wasn't very athletic. I always thought it would have been better, for me, if she was, see. I can talk better to people I can wrestle with. Serious though, I mean about working. And quick like Cathy could think. Only . . ."

Rydra's hand drifted down, then made a jerk motion to the left.

"Only," said Calli, his hand falling from his belly, his breath more easy, "she's got be a whole person, a new person, not somebody who is half what we remember about somebody else."

"Yes," said Ron. "I mean if she's a good navigator, and she loves us."

". . . could love us," said Calli.

"If she was all you wanted and herself besides," asked Rydra, her head shaking between two names on the screen, "could you love her?"

The hesitation, the nod slow from the big man, quick from the boy.

Rydra's hand came down on the crystal face, and the name glowed on the screen. "Mollya Twa, Navigator-One." Her coordinate numbers followed. Rydra dialed them at the desk.

Seventy-five feet overhead something glittered. One among hundreds of thousands of glass coffins was tracking from the wall above them on an inductor beam.

The recall-stage jutted up a pattern of lugs, the tips glowing. The coffin dropped, its contents obscured by streaks and hexagonal bursts of frost inside the glass. The lugs caught the template on the coffin's base. It rocked a moment, settled, clicked.

The frost melted of a sudden, and the inside surface fogged, then ran with droplets. They stepped forward to see.

Dark band on dark. A movement beneath the glaring glass; then the glass parted, melting back from her dark, warm skin and beating, terrified eyes.

"It's all right," Calli said, touching her shoulder. She raised her head to look at his hand, then dropped back to the pillow. Ron crowded the Navigator-Two. "Hello?"

"Eh . . . Miss Twa?" Calli said. "You're alive now. Will you love us?"

"Ninyi ni nani?" Her face was puzzled. *"Nino wapi hapa?"*

Ron looked up amazed. "I don't think she speaks English."

"Yes. I know," Rydra grinned. "But other than that she's perfect. This way you'll have to get to know each other before you can say anything really foolish. She likes to wrestle, Ron.''

Ron looked at the young woman in the case. Her graphite colored hair was natural, her dark lips purpled with chill. "You wrestle?"

"Ninyi ni nani?" she asked again.

Calli lifted his hand from her shoulder and stepped back. Ron scratched his head and frowned.

"Well?" said Rydra.

Calli shrugged. "Well, we don't know."

"Navigation Instruments are standard gear. There won't be any trouble communicating there."

"She is pretty," Ron said. "You are pretty. Don't be frightened. You're alive now."

"Ninaogapa!" She seized Calli's hand. *"Jee, ni usiku au mchana?"* Her eyes were wide.

"Please don't be frightened!" Ron took the wrist of the hand that had seized Calli's.

"Sielewi lugha yenu." She shook her head, a gesture containing no negation, only bewilderment. *"Sikujuweni ninyi nani. Ninaogapa."*

And with bereavement-born urgency, both Ron and Calli nodded in affirmative reassurance.

Rydra stepped between them and spoke.

After a long silence, the woman nodded slowly.

"She says she'll go with you. She lost two-thirds of her triple seven years ago, also killed through the Invasion. That's why she came to the Morgue and killed herself. She says she will go with you. Will you take her?"

"She's still afraid," Ron said. "Please don't be. I won't hurt you. Calli won't hurt."

"If she'll come with us," Calli said, "we'll take her."

The Customs Officer coughed. "Where do I get her psyche rating?"

"Right on the screen under the filing crystal. That's how they're arranged within the larger categories."

The Officer walked back to the crystal. "Well"—He took out his pad and began to record the indices. "It's taken a while but you've got just about everybody."

"Integrate," Rydra said.

He did, and looked up, surprised in spite of himself. "Captain Wong, I think you've got your crew!"

VI

∿∿∿∿∿∿∿∿∿∿∿∿∿∿∿∿∿∿∿∿∿∿∿∿∿∿∿∿∿∿∿

Dear Mocky,

When you get this I'll have taken off two hours ago. It's a half hour before dawn and I want to talk to you, but I won't wake you up again.

I am, nostalgically enough, taking out Fobo's old ship, the Rimbaud *(the name was Muels' idea, remember). At least, I'm familiar with it; lots of good memories here. I leave in twenty minutes.*

Present location: I'm sitting in a folding chair in the freight lock looking over the field. The sky is star speckled to the west, and gray to the east. Black needles of ships pattern around me. Lines of blue signal lights fade toward the south. It is calm now. Subject of my thinking: a hectic night of crew hunting that took me all over Transport Town and out to the Morgue, through dives and glittering byways, etc. Loud and noisy at the beginning, calming to this at the end.

To get a good pilot you watch him wrestle. A trained captain can tell exactly what sort of a pilot a person will make by observing his reflexes in the arena. Only I am not that well trained.

Remember what you said about muscle-reading? Maybe you were righter than you thought. Last night I ran into a kid, a Navigator, who looks like Brancusi's graduation offering, or maybe what Michelangelo wished the human body was. He was born in Transport and knows pilot wrestling inside out, apparently. So I watched him watch my pilot

*wrestle, and just looking at his quivers and jerks I
got a complete analysis of what was going on over
my head.*

*You know De Faure's theory that psychic indi-
ces have their corresponding muscular tensions (a
restatement of the old Wilhelm Reich hypothesis of
muscular armature): I was thinking about it last
night. The kid I was telling you about was part of a
broken triple, two guys and a girl and the girl got it
from the Invaders. The boys made me want to cry.
But I didn't. Instead I took them to the Morgue and
found them a replacement. Weird business. I'm sure
they'll think it was magic for the rest of their lives.
The basic requirements, however, were all on file: a
female Navigator-One who lacks two men. How to
adjust the indices? I read Ron's and Calli's from
watching them move while they talked. The corpses
are filed under psyche-indices so I just had to feel
out when they were congruent. The final choice was
a stroke of genius, if I do say so. I had it down to
six young ladies who would do. But it needed to be
more precise than that, and I couldn't play it more
precise, at least not by ear. One young lady was
from N'gonda Province in Pan Africa. She'd suicided
seven years ago. Lost two husbands in an Invasion
attack, and returned to earth in the middle of an
embargo. You remember what the politics were like
then between Pan Africa and Americasia; I was
sure she didn't speak English. We woke her, and she
didn't. Now, at this point, their indices may be a
mite jarring. But, by the time they fight through
learning to understand each other—and they will,
because they need to—they'll graph out congruent a
foot down the logarithmic grid. Clever?*

*And Babel-17, the real reason for this letter.
Told you I had deciphered it enough to know where
the next attack will be. The Alliance War Yards at
Armsedge. Wanted to let you know that's where I'm
going, just in case. Talk and talk and talk: what
sort of mind can talk like that language talks? And*

*why? Still scared—like a kid at a spelling bee—but
having fun. My platoon reported an hour ago.
Crazy, lazy lovable kids all. In just a few minutes
I'll be going to see my Slug (fat galoof with black
eyes, hair, beard; moves slow and thinks fast). You
know, Mocky, getting this crew together I was interested in one thing (above competency, and they are
all competent): they had to be people I could talk
to. And I can.*

Love, Rydra.

VII

Light but no shadow. The General stood up on the
saucer-sled, looking at the black ship, the paling sky. At the
base he stepped from the gliding two-foot diameter disk,
climbed onto the lift, and rose a hundred feet toward the lock.
She wasn't in the captain's cabin. He ran into a fat bearded
man who directed him up the corridor to the freight lock. He
climbed to the top of the ladder and took hold of his breath
because it was about to run away.

She dropped her feet from the wall, sat up in the canvas
chair and smiled. "General Forester, I thought I might see
you this morning." She folded a piece of message tissue and
sealed the edge.

"I wanted see you . . ." and his breath was gone and had
to be caught once more, "before you left."

"I wanted to see you, too."

"You told me if I gave you license to conduct this
expedition, you would inform me where you———"

"My report, which you should find satisfactory, was
mailed last night and is on your desk at Administrative
Alliance Headquarters—or will be in an hour."

"Oh. I see."

She smiled. "You'll have to go shortly. We take off in a few minutes."

'Yes. Actually, I'm taking off for Administrative Alliance Headquarters myself this morning, so I was here at the field, and I'd already gotten a synopsis of your report by stellarphone a few minutes ago, and I just wanted to say——" and he said nothing.

"General Forester, once I wrote a poem I'm reminded of. It was called 'Advice to Those Who Would Love Poets'."

The General opened his teeth without separating his lips.

"It started something like:

> *Young man, she will gnaw out your tongue. Lady,*
> *he will steal your hands . . .*

You can read the rest. It's in my second book. If you're not willing to lose a poet seven times a day, it's frustrating as hell."

He said simply: "You knew I . . ."

"I knew and I know. And I'm glad."

The lost breath returned and an unfamiliar thing was happening to his face: he smiled. "When I was a private, Miss Wong, and we'd be confined to barracks, we'd talk about girls and girls and girls. And somebody would say about one: she was so pretty she didn't have to give me any, just promise me some." He let the stiffness leave his shoulders a moment, and though they actually fell half an inch, the effect was that they seemed broader by two. "That's what I was feeling."

"Thank you for telling me," she said. "I like you, General. And I promise I'll still like you the next time I see you."

"I . . . thank you. I guess that's all. Just thank you . . . for knowing and promising." Then he said, "I have to go now, don't I?"

"We'll be taking off in ten minutes."

"Your letter," he said, "I'll mail it for you."

"Thanks." She handed it to him, he took her hand, and for the slightest moment with the slightest pressure, held her. Then he turned, left. Minutes later she watched his saucer-sled glide across the concrete, its sun-side flaring suddenly as light blistered the east.

PART TWO

~~~~~~

Ver Dorco

If words are paramount I am afraid
that words are all my hands have ever seen . . .

—from *Quartet*

1

‚‚

The retranscribed material passed on the sorting screen.
By the computer console lay the four pages of definitions she
had amassed and a *cuaderno* full of grammatical speculations.
Chewing her lower lip, she ran through the frequency tabulation
of depressed diphthongs. On the wall she had tacked three
charts labeled:

Possible Phonemic Structure . . .
Possible Phonetic Structure . . .
Semiotic, Semantic, and Syntactic Ambiguities . . .

The last contained the problems to be solved. The
questions, formulated and answered, were transferred as cer-
tainties to the first two.

"Captain?"

She turned on the bubble seat.

Hanging from the entrance hatch by his knees was
Diavalo.

"Yes?"

"What you want for dinner?" The little platoon cook
was a boy of seventeen. Two cosmetisurgical horns jutted
from shocked albino hair. He was scratching one ear with the
tip of his tail.

Rydra shrugged. "No preferences. Check around with
the rest of the platoon."

"Those guys'll eat liquified organic waste if I give it to
them. No imagination, Captain. What about pheasant under
glass, or maybe rock Cornish game hen?"

"You're in the mood for poultry?"

"Well——" He released the bar with one knee and kicked the wall so he swung back and forth. "I could go for something birdy."

"If nobody objects, try coq au vin, baked Idahos, and broiled beefsteak tomatoes."

"Now you're cookin'!"

"Strawberry shortcake for dessert?"

Diavalo snapped his fingers and swung up toward the hatch. Rydra laughed and turned back to the console.

"Macon on the coq, May wine with the meal!" The pink-eyed face was gone.

Rydra had discovered the third example of what might have been syncope when the bubble chair sagged back. The cuaderno slammed against the edge of the desk. Her shoulders wrenched. Behind her the skin of the bubble chair split and showered suspended silicon.

The cabin stilled and she turned to see Diavalo spin through the hatch and crack his hip as he grabbed at the transparent wall.

Jerk.

She slipped on the wet, deflated skin of the bubble chair. The Slug's face jounced on the intercom. "Captain!"

"What the hell . . . !" she demanded.

The blinker from Drive Maintenance was flashing. Something jarred the ship again.

"Are we still breathing?"

"Just a . . ." The Slug's face, heavy and rimmed with a thin black beard, got an unpleasant expression. "Yes. Air: all right. Drive Maintenance has the problem."

"If those damn kids have . . ." She clicked them on.

Flip, the platoon Maintenance Foreman, said, "Jesus, Captain, something blew."

"What?"

"I don't know." Flop's face appeared over his shoulder.

"A and B shifters are all right. C's glittering like a Fourth of July sparkler. Where the hell are we, anyway?"

"On the first hour shift between Earth and Luna. We haven't even got free of Stellarcenter-9. Navigation?" Another click.

Mollya's dark face popped up.

"Wie gehts?" demanded Rydra.

The first Navigator reeled off their probability curve and located them between two vague logarithmic spirals. "We're orbiting Earth so far," Ron's voice cut over. "Something knocked us way off course. We don't have any drive power and we're just drifting."

"How high up and how fast?"

"Calli's trying to find out now."

"I'm going to take a look around outside." She called down to the Sensory Detail. "Nose, what does it smell like out there?"

"It stinks. Nothing in this range. We've hit soup."

"Can you hear anything, Ear?"

"Not a peep, Captain. All the stasis currents in this area are at a standstill. We're too near a large gravitational mass. There's a faint ethric undertow about fifty spectres K-ward. But I don't think it will take us anywhere except around in a circle. We're riding in momentum from the last stiff wind from Earth's magnosphere."

"What's it look like, Eyes?"

"Inside of a coal scuttle. Whatever happened to us, we picked a dead spot to have it happen in. In my range that undertow is a little stronger and might move us into a good tide."

Brass cut in. "But I'd like to know where it's going before I went jum'ing off into it. That means I gotta know where we are, first."

"Navigation?"

Silence for a moment. Then the three faces appeared. Calli said, "We don't know, Captain."

The gravity field had stabilized a few degrees off. The silicon suspension collected in one corner. Little Diavalo shook his head and blinked. Through the contortion of pain on his face he whispered, "What happened, Captain?"

"Damned if I know," Rydra said. "But I'm going to find out."

Dinner was eaten silently. The platoon, all kids under twenty-one, made as little noise as possible. At the officers' table the Navigators sat across from the apparitional figures of the discorporate Sensory Observers. The hefty Slug at the table's head poured wine for the silent crew. Rydra dined with Brass.

"I don't know." He shook his maned head, turning his glass in gleaming claws. "It was smooth sailing with nothing in the way. Whatever ha''ened, ha''ened inside the shi'."

Diavalo, hip in a pressure bandage, dourfully brought in the shortcake, served Rydra and Brass, then retired to his seat at the platoon table.

"So," Rydra said, "we're orbiting Earth with all our instruments knocked out and can't even tell where we are."

"The hy'erstasis instruments are good," he reminded her. "We just don't know where we are on this side of the jum'."

"And we can't jump if we don't know where we're jumping from." She looked over the dining room. "Do you think they're expecting to get out of this, Brass?"

"They're ho'ing you can get them out, Ca'tain."

She touched the rim of her glass to her lower lip.

"If somebody doesn't, we'll sit here eating Diavalo's good food for six months, then suffocate. We can't even get a signal out until after we lea' for hy'erstasis with the regular communicator shorted. I asked the Navigators to see if they could im'rovise something, but no go. They just had time to see that we were launched in a great circle."

"We should have windows," Rydra said. "At least we could look out at the stars and time our orbit. It can't be more than a couple of hours."

Brass nodded. "Shows you what modern conveniences mean. A 'orthole and an old-fashioned sextant could set us right, but we're electronicized to the gills, and here we sit, with a neatly insoluble 'roblem."

"Circling——" Rydra put down her wine.

"What is it?"

"Der Kreis," said Rydra. She frowned.

"What's that?" asked Brass.

"Ratas, orbis, il cerchio." She put her palms flat on the table top and pressed. "Circles," she said. "Circles in different languages!"

Brass' confusion was terrifying through his fangs. The glinting fleece above his eyes bristled.

"Sphere," she said, "il globo, gumlas." She stood up, "Kule, kuglet, kring!"

"Does it matter what language it's in? A circle is a cir——"

But she was laughing, running from the dining room.

In her cabin she grabbed up her translation. Her eyes fled down the pages. She banged the button for the Navigators. Ron, wiping whipped-cream from his mouth, said, "Yes, Captain? What do you want?"

"A watch," said Rydra, "and a—bag of marbles!"

"Huh?" asked Calli.

"You can finish your shortcake later. Meet me in G-center right now."

"Mar-bles?" articulated Mollya wonderingly. "Marbles?"

"One of the kids in the platoon must have brought along a bag of marbles. Get it and meet me in G-center."

She jumped over the ruined skin of the bubble seat and leapt up the hatchway, turned off at the radial shaft seven, and launched down the cylindrical corridor toward the hollow spherical chamber of G-center. The calculated center of gravity of the ship, it was a chamber thirty feet in diameter in constant free fall where certain gravity-sensitive instruments took their readings. A moment later the three Navigators appeared through triametric entrances. Ron held up a mesh bag of glass balls. "Lizzy asks you to try and get these back to her by tomorrow afternoon because she's been challenged by the kids in Drive and she wants to keep her championship."

"If this works she can probably have them back to-night."

"Work?" Mollya wanted to know. "Idea you?"

"I do. Only it's not really my idea."

"Whose is it, and what is it?" Ron asked.

"I suppose it belongs to somebody who speaks another language. What we've got to do is arrange the marbles around the wall of the room in a perfect sphere, and then sit back with the clock and keep tabs on the second hand."

"What for?" asked Calli.

"To see where they go and how long it takes them to get there."

"I don't get it," said Ron.

"Our orbit tends toward a great circle about the Earth, right? That means everything in the ship is also tending to orbit in a great circle, and, if left free of influence, will automatically seek out such a path."

"Right. So what?"

"Help me get these marbles in place," Rydra said. "These things have iron cores. Magnetize the walls, will you, to hold them in place, so they can all be released at once." Ron, confused, went to power the metal walls of the spherical chamber. "You still don't see? You're mathematicians, tell me about great circles."

Calli took a handful of marbles and started to space them—tiny click after click—over the wall. "A great circle is the largest circle you can cut through a sphere."

"The diameter of the great circle equals the diameter of the sphere," from Ron, as he came back from the power switch.

"The summation of the angles of intersection of any three great circles within one topologically contained shape approaches five hundred and forty degrees. The summation of the angles of N great circles approaches N times one hundred and eighty degrees." Mollya intoned the definitions, which she had begun memorizing in English with the help of a personafix that morning, with her musically inflected voice. "Marble here, yes?"

"All over, yes. Evenly as you can space them, but they don't have to be exact. Tell me some more about the intersections."

"Well," said Ron, "on any given sphere all great circles intersect each other—or lie congruent."

Rydra laughed. "Just like that, hey? Are there any other circles on a sphere that have to intersect no matter how you maneuver them?"

"I think you can push around any other circles so that they're equidistant at all points and don't touch. All great circles have to have at least two points in common."

"Think about that for a minute and look at these marbles, all being pulled along great circles."

Mollya suddenly floated back from the wall with an expression of recognition and brought her hands together. She blurted something in Kiswahili, and Rydra laughed. "That's right," she said. To Ron's and Calli's bewilderment she translated: "They'll move toward each other and their paths'll intersect."

Calli's eyes widened. "That's right, at exactly a quarter of the way around our orbit, they should have flattened out to a circular plane."

"Lying along the plane of our orbit," Ron finished.

Mollya frowned and made a stretching motion with her hands. "Yeah," Ron said, "a distorted circular plain with a tail at each end, from which we can compute which way the earth lies."

"Clever, huh?" Rydra moved back into the corridor opening. "I figure we can do this once, then fire our rockets enough to blast us maybe seventy or eighty miles either up or down without hurting anything. From that we can get the length of our orbits, as well as our speed. That'll be all the information we need to locate ourselves in relation to the nearest major gravitational influence. From there we can jump stasis. All our communications instruments for stasis are in working order. We can signal for help and pull in some replacements from a stasis station."

The amazed Navigators joined her in the corridor. "Count down," Rydra said.

At zero Ron released the magnetic walls. Slowly the marbles began to drift, lining up slowly.

"Guess you learn something every day," Calli said. "If you'd asked me, I would have said we were stuck here forever. And knowing things like this is supposed to be my job. Where did you get the idea?"

"From the word for 'great circle' in . . . another language."

"Language speaking tongue?" Mollya asked. "You mean?"

"Well," Rydra took out a metal tracing plate and a stylus. "I'm simplifying it a little, but let me show you." She marked the plate. "Let's say the word for circle is: O. This language has a melody system to illustrate comparatives. We'll represent this by the diacritical marks: ˇ, ‾, and ˆ, respectively, mean smallest, ordinary, and biggest. So what would Ŏ mean?''

"Smallest possible circle?" said Calli. "That's a single point."

Rydra nodded. "Now, when referring to a circle on a sphere, suppose the word for just an ordinary circle is Ō followed by either of two symbols, one of which means not touching anything else, the other of which means crossing —11 or X. What would ŌX mean?''

"Ordinary circle that intersects," said Ron.

"And because all great circles intersect, in this language the word for great circle is always ÔX. It carries the information right in the word. Just like *busstop* or *foxhole* carry information in English that *la gare* or *le terrier*—comparable words in French—lack. "Great Circle" carries some information with it, but not the right information to get us out of the jam we're in. We have to go to another language in order to think about the problem clearly without going through all sorts of roundabout paths for the proper aspects of what we want to deal with.''

"What language is this?" asked Calli.

"I don't know its real name. For now it's called Babel-17. From what little I know about it already, most of its words carry more information about the things they refer to than any four or five languages I know put together, and in less space." She gave a brief translation for Mollya.

"Who speak?" Mollya asked, determined to stick to her minimal English.

Rydra bit the inside of her lip. When she asked herself that question, her stomach would tighten, her hands start toward something and the yearning for an answer grow nearly to pain in the back of her throat. It happened now; it faded. "I don't know. But I wish I did. That's what the main reason for this trip is, to find out."

"Babel-17," Ron repeated.

One of the platoon tube-boys coughed behind them.

"What is it, Carlos?"

Squat, taurine, with a lot of curly black hair, Carlos had

big, loose muscles, and a slight lisp. "Captain, could I show you something?" He shifted from side to side in adolescent awkwardness, scuffing his bare soles, heat-callused from climbing over the drive tubes, against the door sill. "Something down in the tubes. I think you should take a look at it yourself."

"Did Slug tell you to get me?"

Carlos prodded behind his ear with a gnawed thumbnail. "Um-hm."

"You three can take care of this business, can't you?"

"Sure, Captain." Calli looked at the closing marbles.

Rydra ducked after Carlos. They rode down the ladder-lift and hunched through the low ceilinged causeway.

"Down here," Carlos said, hesitantly taking the lead beneath arched bus bars. At a mesh platform he stopped and opened a component cabinet in the wall. "See." He removed a board of printed circuits. "There." A thin crack ran across the plastic surface. "It's been broken."

"How?" Rydra asked.

"Like this." He took the plate in both hands and made a bending gesture.

"Sure it didn't crack by itself?"

"It can't," Carlos said. "When it's in place, it's supported too well. You couldn't crack it with a sledge hammer. This panel carries all the communication circuits."

Rydra nodded.

"The gyroscopic field deflectors for all our regular space maneuvering..." He opened another door and took out another panel. "Here."

Rydra ran her fingernail along the crack in the second plate. "Someone in the ship broke these," she said. "Take them to the shop. Tell Lizzy when she finishes reprinting them to bring them to me and I'll put them in. I'll give her the marbles back then."

II

Drop a gem in thick oil. The brilliance yellows slowly, ambers, goes red at last, dies. That was the leap into hyperstatic space.

At the computer console, Rydra pondered the charts. The dictionary had doubled since the trip began. Satisfaction filled one side of her mind like a good meal. Words, and their easy patterning, facile always on her tongue, in her fingers, ordered themselves for her, revealing, defining, and revealing.

And there was a traitor. The question, a vacuum where no information would come to answer who or what or why, made an emptiness on the other side of her brain, agonizing to collapse. Someone had deliberately broken those plates. Lizzy said so, too. What words for this? The names of the entire crew, and by each, a question mark.

Fling a jewel into a glut of jewels. This is the leap out of hyperstasis into the area of the Alliance War Yards at Armsedge.

At the communication board, she put on the Sensory Helmet. "Do you want to translate for me?"

The indicator light blinked acceptance. Each discorporate observer perceived the details of the gravitational and electromagnetic flux of the stasis currents for a certain frequency with all his senses, each in his separate range. Those details were myriad, and the pilot sailed the ship through those currents as sailing ships winded the liquid ocean. But the helmet made a condensation that the captain could view for a general survey of the matrix, reduced to terms that would leave the corporate viewer sane.

She opened the helmet, covering her eyes, ears, and nose.

Flung through loops of blue and wrung with indigo, drifted the complex of stations and planetoids making up the War Yards. A musical hum punctured with bursts of static sounded over the earphones. The olfactory emitters gave a confused odor of perfumes and hot oil charged with the bitter smell of burning citrus peel. With three of her senses filled, she was loosed from the reality of the cabin to drift through sensory abstractions. It took nearly a minute to collect her sensations, to begin their interpretation.

"All right. What am I looking at?"

"The lights are the various planetoids and ring stations that make up the War Yards," the Eye explained to her. "That bluish color to the left is a radar net they have spread out toward Stellarcenter Forty-two. Those red flashes in the upper right hand corner are just a reflection of Bellatrix from a half-glazed solar-disk rotating four degrees outside your field of vision."

"What's that low humming?" Rydra asked.

"The ship's drive," the Ear explained. "Just ignore it. I'll block it out if you want."

Rydra nodded, and the hum ceased.

"That clicking——" the Ear began.

"—is morse code," Rydra finished. "I recognize that. It must be two radio amateurs that want to keep off the visual circuits."

"That's right," the Ear confirmed.

"What stinks like that?"

"The overall smell is just Bellatrix's gravitational field. You can't receive the olfactory sensations in stereo, but the burnt lemon peel is the power plant that's located in that green glare right ahead of you."

"Where do we dock?"

"In the sound of the E-minor triad."

"In the hot oil you can smell bubbling to your left."

"Home in on that white circle."

Rydra switched to the pilot. "O.K., Brass, take her in."

The saucer-disk slid down the ramp as she balanced easily in the four-fifths gravity. A breeze through the artificial twilight pushed her hair back from her shoulders. Around her stretched the major arsenal of the Alliance. Momentarily she pondered the accident of birth that had seated her firmly inside the Alliance's realm. Born a galaxy away, she might as easily have been an Invader. Her poems were popular on both sides. That was upsetting. She put the thought away. Here, gliding the Alliance War Yards, it was not clever to be upset over that.

"Captain Wong, you come under the auspices of General Forester."

She nodded as her saucer stopped.

"He forwarded us information that you are at present the expert on Babel-17."

She nodded once more. Now the other saucer paused before hers.

"I'm very happy then, to meet you, and for any assistance I can offer, please ask."

She extended her hand. "Thank you, Baron Ver Dorco."

Black eyebrows raised and the slash of mouth curved in the dark face. "You read heraldry?" He raised long fingers to the shield on his chest.

"I do."

"An accomplishment, Captain. We live in a world of isolated communities, each hardly touching its neighbor, each speaking, as it were, a different language."

"I speak many."

The Baron nodded. "Sometimes I believe, Captain Wong, that without the Invasion, something for the Alliance to focus its energies upon, our society would disintegrate. Captain Wong——" He stopped, and the fine lines of his face shifted, contracted to concentration, then a sudden opening. "Rydra Wong . . . ?"

She nodded, smiling at his smile, yet wary before what the recognition would mean.

"I didn't realize——" He extended his hand as though he were meeting her all over again. "But, of course——" The surface of his manner shaled away, and had she never seen this transformation before she would have warmed to his warmth. "Your books, I want you to know——" The sentence trailed in a slight shaking of the head. Dark eyes too wide; lips, in their humor, too close to a leer; hands seeking one another: it all spoke to her of a disquieting appetite for her presence, a hunger for something she was or might be, a ravenous—"Dinner at my house is served at seven." He interrupted her thought with unsettling appropriateness. "You will dine with the Baroness and myself this evening."

"Thank you. But I wanted to discuss with my crew——"

"I extend the invitation to your entire entourage. We have a spacious house, conference rooms at your disposal, as well as entertainment, certainly less confined than your ship." The tongue, purplish and flickering behind white, white teeth; the brown lines of his lips, she thought, form words as languidly as the slow mandibles of the cannibal mantis.

"Please come a little early so we can prepare you——"

She caught her breath, then felt foolish; a faint narrowing of his eyes told her he had registered, though not understood, her start.

"—for your tour through the yards. General Forester has suggested you be made privy to all our efforts against the Invaders. That is quite an honor, Madam. There are many well-seasoned officers at the yards who have not seen some of the things you will be shown. A good deal of it will probably be tedious, I dare say. In my opinion, it's stuffing you with a lot of trivial tidbits. But some of our attempts have been rather ingenious. We keep our imaginations simmering."

This man brings out the paranoid in me, she thought. I don't like him. "I'd prefer not to impose on you, Baron. There are some matters on my ship that I must——"

"Do come. Your work here will be much facilitated if you accept my hospitality, I assure you. A woman of your talent and accomplishment would be an honor to my house. And recently I have been starved"—dark lips slid together over gleaming teeth—"for intelligent conversation."

She felt her jaw clamp involuntarily on a third ceremonious refusal. But the Baron was saying: "I will expect you, and your crew, leisurely, before seven."

The saucer-disk slid away over the concourse. Rydra looked back at the ramp where her ship waited, silhouetted against the false evening. Her disk began to negotiate the slope back to the *Rimbaud*.

"Well," she said to the little albino cook who had just come out of his pressure bandage the day before, "you're off tonight. Slug, the crew's going out to dinner. See if you can brush the kids up on their table manners—make sure every one knows which knife to eat his peas with, and all that."

"The salad fork is the little one on the outside," the Slug announced suavely, turning to the platoon.

"And what about the little one outside that?" Allegra asked.

"That's for oysters."

"But suppose they don't serve oysters?"

Flop rubbed his underlip with the knuckle of his thumb. "I guess you could pick your teeth with it."

Brass dropped a paw on Rydra's shoulder. "How you feel, Ca'tain?"

"Like a pig over a barbecue pit."

"You look sort of done——" Calli began.

"Done?" she asked.

"—in," he finished, quizzically.

"Maybe I've been working too hard. We're guests at the Baron Ver Dorco's this evening. I suppose we can all relax a bit there."

"Ver Dorco?" asked Mollya.

"He's in charge of coordinating the various research projects against the Invaders."

"This is where they make all the bigger and better secret weapons?" Ron asked.

"They also make smaller, more deadly ones. I imagine it should be an education."

"These sabotage attem'ts," Brass said. She had given them a rough idea of what was going on. "A successful one here at the War Yards could be 'retty bad to our efforts against the Invaders."

"It's about as central a hit as they could try, next to planting a bomb in Administrative Alliance Headquarters itself."

"Will you be able to stop it?" Slug asked.

Rydra shrugged, turning to the simmering absences of

the discorporate crew. "I've got a couple of ideas. Look, I'm going to ask you guys to be sort of unhospitable this evening and do some spying. Eyes, I want you to stay on the ship and make sure you're the only one here. Ears, once we leave for the Baron's, go invisible and from then on, don't get more than six feet away from me until we're all back to the ship. Nose, you run messages back and forth. There's something going on that I don't like. I don't know whether it's my imagination or what."

The Eye spoke something ominous. Ordinarily the corporate could only converse with the discorporate—and remember the conversation—over special equipment. Rydra solved the problem by immediately translating whatever they spoke to her into Basque before the weak synapses broke. Though the original words were lost, the translation remained: Those broken circuit plates weren't your imagination, was the gist of the Basque she retained.

She looked over the crew with gnawing discomfort. If one of the kids or officers was merely psychotically destructive, it would show up on his psyche index. There was, among them, a consciously destructive one. It hurt, like an unlocateable splinter in the sole of her foot that jabbed occasionally with the pressure of walking. She remembered how she had searched them from the night. Pride. Warm pride in the way their functions meshed as they moved her ship through the stars. The warmth was the relieved anticipation for all that could go wrong with the machine-called-the-ship, if the machine-called-the-crew were not interlocked and precise. Cool pride in another part of her mind, at the ease with which they moved by one another: the kids, inexperienced both in living and working; the adults, so near pressure situations that might have scarred their polished efficiency and made psychic burrs to snag one another. But she had chosen them; and the ship, her world, was a beautiful place to walk, work, live, for a journey's length.

But there was a traitor.

That shorted something. *Somewhere in Eden, now . . .* she recalled, again looking over the crew. *Somewhere in Eden, now, a worm, a worm.* Those cracked plates told her: the worm wanted to destroy not just her, but the ship, its crew, and contents, slowly. No blades plunged in the night, no shots from around a corner, no cord looped on the throat as she entered a dark cabin. Babel-17, how good a language would it be to argue with for your life?

"Slug, the Baron wants me to come soon and see some of his latest methods of slaughter. Have the kids there decently early, will you? I'm leaving now. Eye and Ear, hop aboard."

"Righto, Captain," from Slug.

The discorporate crew deperceptualized.

She leaned her sled over the ramp again and slid away from the milling youngsters and officers, curious at the source of her apprehension.

III

~~~~~~

"Gross, uncivilized weapons." The Baron gestured toward the row of plastic cylinders increasing in size along the rack. "It's a shame to waste time on such clumsy contraptions. The little one there can demolish an area of about fifty square miles. The big ones leave a crater twenty-seven miles deep and a hundred and fifty across. Barbaric. I frown on their use. That one on the left is more subtle: it explodes once with enough force to demolish a good size building, but the bomb casing itself is hidden and unhurt under the rubble. Six hours later it explodes again and does the damage of a fair-sized atomic bomb. This leaves the victims enough time to concentrate their reclamation forces, all sorts of reconstruction workers, Red Cross nurses, or whatever the Invaders call them, lots of experts determining the size of the damage. Then *poof*. A delayed hydrogen explosion, and a good thirty or forty miles crater. It doesn't do as much physical damage as even the smallest of these others, but it gets rid of a lot of equipment and busybody do-gooders. Still, a schoolboy's weapon. I keep them in my own personal collection just to show them we have standard fare.''

She followed him through the archway into the next hall. There were filing cabinets along the wall and a single display case in the center of the room.

"Now here is one I'm justly proud of." The Baron walked to the case and the transparent walls fell apart.

"What," Rydra asked, "exactly is it?"

"What does it look like?"

"A . . . piece of rock."

"A chunk of metal," corrected the Baron.

"Is it explosive, or particularly hard?"

"It won't go bang," he assured her. "Its tensile strength is a bit over titanium steel, but we have much harder plastics."

Rydra started to extend her hand, then thought to ask, "May I pick it up and examine it?"

"I doubt it," the Baron said. "Try."

"What will happen?"

"See for yourself."

She reached out to take the dull chunk. Her hand closed on air two inches above the surface. She moved her fingers down to touch it, but they came together inches to the side. Rydra frowned.

She moved her hand to the left, but it was on the other side of the strange shard.

"Just a moment." The Baron smiled, picked up the fragment. "Now if you saw this just lying on the ground, you wouldn't look twice, would you?"

"Poisonous?" Rydra suggested. "Is it a component of something else?"

"No." The Baron turned the shape about thoughtfully. "Just highly selective. And obliging." He raised his hand. "Suppose you needed a gun''—in the Baron's hand now was a sleek vibra-gun of a model later than she had ever seen—"or a crescent wrench." Now he held a foot long wrench. He adjusted the opening. "Or a machete." The blade glistened as he waved his arm back. "Or a small crossbow." It had a pistol grip and a bow length of not quite ten inches. The spring, however, was doubled back on itself and held with quarter inch bolts. The Baron pulled the trigger—there was no arrow—and the *thump* of the release, followed by the continuous *pinnnnnng* of the vibrating tensile bar, set her teeth against one another.

"It's some sort of illusion," Rydra said. "That's why I couldn't touch it."

"A metal punch," said the Baron. It appeared in his hand, a hammer with a particularly thick head. He swung it against the floor of the case that had held the "weapon" with a strident clang. "There."

Rydra saw the circular indentation left by the hammer-head. Raised in the middle was the faint shape of the Ver Dorco shield. She moved the tips of her fingers over the bossed metal, still warm from impact.

"No illusion," said the Baron. "That crossbow will put a six inch shaft completely through three inches of oak at forty yards. And the vibra-gun—I'm sure you know what it can do."

He held the—it was a chunk of metal again—above its stand in the case. "Put it back for me."

She stretched her hand beneath his, and he dropped the chunk. Her fingers closed to grab it. But it was on the stand again.

"No hocus-pocus. Merely selective and . . . obliging."

He touched the edge of the case and the plastic sides closed over the display. "A clever plaything. Let's look at something else."

"But how does it work?"

Ver Dorco smiled. "We've managed to polarize alloys of the heavier elements so that they exist only on certain perceptual matrices. Otherwise, they deflect. That means that, besides visually—and we can blank that out as well—it's undetectable. No weight, no volume; all it has is inertia. Which means simply by carrying it aboard any hyperstasis craft, you'll put its drive controls out of commission. Two or three grams of this anywhere near the inertia-stasis system will create all sorts of unaccounted-for strain. That's its major function right there. Smuggle that on board the Invaders' ships and we can stop worrying about them. The rest—that's child's play. An unexpected property of polarized matter is tensile-memory." They moved toward an archway into the next room. "Annealed in any shape for a time, and codified, the structure of that shape is retained down to the molecules. At any angle to the direction that the matter has been polarized in, each molecule has completely free movement. Just jar it, and it falls into that structure like a rubber figure returning to shape." The Baron glanced back at the case. "Simple, really. There"—he motioned toward the filing cabinets along the wall—"is the real weapon: approximately three thousand individual plans incorporating that little polarized chunk. The 'weapon' is the knowledge of what to do with what you have. In hand-to-hand combat, a six-inch length of vanadium wire can be deadly. Inserted directly into the inner corner of the eye, piercing diagonally across the frontal lobes, then brought quickly down, it punctures the cerebellum, causing general paralysis; thrust completely in, and it will mangle the joint of spinal cord and the medulla: Death. You can use the same piece of wire to short out a Type 27-QX communications unit, which is the sort currently employed in the Invaders' stasis systems."

Rydra felt the muscles along her spine tighten. The repulsion which she had quelled till now came flooding back.

"This next display is from the Borgia. The Borgia," he laughed, "my nickname for our toxicology department. Again, some terribly gross products." He picked a sealed glass phial from a wall rack. "Pure diphtheria toxin. Enough here to make the reservoir of a good-sized city fatal."

"But standard vaccination procedure——" Rydra began.

"Diphtheria toxin, my dear. Toxin! Back when contagious diseases were a problem, you know, they would examine the corpses of diphtheria victims and discover nothing but a few hundred thousand baccilli, all in the victim's throat. Nowhere else. With any other sort of bacillis, that's enough of an infection to cause a minor cough. It took years to discover what was going on. That tiny number of bacilli produced an even tinier bit of a substance that is still the most deadly natural organic compound we know of. The amount required to kill a man—oh, I'd even say thirty or forty men—is, for all practical purposes, undetectable. Up till now, even with all our advances, the only way you could obtain it was from an obliging diphtheria bacillus. The Borgia has changed that.'' He pointed to another bottle. ''Cyanide, the old war horse! But then, the telltale smell of almonds—are you hungry? We can go up for cocktails any time you wish.''

She shook her head, quickly and firmly.

''Now these are delicious. Catalytics.'' He moved his hand from one phial to the next. ''Color blindness, total blindness, tone deafness, complete deafness, ataxia, amnesia, and on and on.'' He dropped his hand and smiled like a hungry rodent. ''And they're all controlled by this. You see, the problem with anything of such a specific effect is that you have to introduce comparatively huge amounts of it. All these require at least a tenth of a gram or more. So, catalytics. None of what I've shown you would have any effect at all even if you swallowed the whole vial.'' He lifted the last container he had pointed to and pressed a stud at the end and there was a faint hiss of escaping gas. ''Until now. A perfectly harmless atomized steroid.''

''Only it activates the poisons here to produce . . . these effects?''

''Exactly,'' smiled the Baron. ''And the catalyst can be in doses nearly as microscopic as the diphtheria toxin. The contents of that blue jar will give you a mild stomach ache and minor head pains for half an hour. Nothing more. The green one beside it: total cerebral atrophy over a period of a week. The victim becomes a living vegetable the rest of his life. The purple one: death.'' He raised his hands, palms up, and laughed. ''I'm famished.'' The hands dropped. ''Shall we go up to dinner?''

Ask him what's in that room over there, she said to herself, and would have dismissed the passing curiosity, but she was thinking in Basque: it was a message from her discorporate bodyguard, invisible beside her.

''When I was a child, Baron''—she moved toward the door—''soon after I came to Earth, I was taken to the circus. It was the first time I had ever seen so many things so close together that were so fascinating. I wouldn't go home till almost an hour after they had intended to leave. What do you have in this room?''

Surprise in the little movement in the muscles of his forehead.

''Show me.''

He bowed his head in mocking, semi-formal aquiescence. ''Modern warfare can be fought on so many delightfully different levels,'' he continued, walking back to her side as if no interruption of the tour had been suggested. ''One wins a battle by making sure one's troops have enough blunderbusses and battle axes like the ones you saw in the first room; or by the well-placed six-inch length of vanadium wire in a Type 27-QX communications unit. With the proper orders delayed, the encounter never takes place. Hand-to-hand weapons, survival kit, plus training, room, and board: three thousand credits per enlisted stellarman over a period of two years active duty. For a garrison of fifteen hundred men that's an outlay of four million, five hundred credits. That same garrison will live in and fight from three hyperstasis battle-ships which, fully-equipped, run about a million and a half credits apiece—a total outlay of nine million credits. We have spent, on occasion, perhaps as much as a million on the preparation of a single spy or saboteur. That is rather higher than usual. And I can't believe a six-inch length of vanadium wire costs a third of a cent. War is costly. And although it has taken some time, Administrative Alliance Headquarters is beginning to realize subtlety pays. This way, Miss—Captain Wong.''

Again they were in a room with only a single display case, but it was seven feet high.

A statue, Rydra thought. No, real flesh, with detail of muscle and joint; no, it must be a statue because a human body, dead or in suspended animation, doesn't look that—alive. Only art could produce that vibrancy.

''So you see, the proper spy is very important.'' Though the door had opened automatically, the Baron held it with his hand in vestigial politeness. ''This is one of our more expensive models. Still well under a million credits, but one of my favourites—though in practice he has his faults.

With a few minor alterations I would like to make him a permanent part of our arsenal."

"A model of a spy?" Rydra asked. "Some sort of robot or android?"

"Not at all." They approached the display case. "We made half a dozen TW-55's. It took the most exacting genetic search. Medical science has progressed so that all sorts of hopeless human refuse lives and reproduces at a frightening rate—inferior creatures that would have been too weak to survive a handful of centuries ago. We chose our parents carefully, and then with artificial insemination we got our half dozen zygotes, three male, three female. We raised them in, oh, such a carefully controlled nutrient environment, speeding the growth rate by hormones and other things. But the beauty of it was the experiential imprinting. Gorgeously healthy creatures; you have no idea how much care they received."

"I once spent a summer on a cattle farm," Rydra said shortly.

The Baron's nod was brisk. "We'd used the experiential imprints before, so we knew what we were doing. But never to synthesize completely the life situation of, say, a sixteen-year-old human. Sixteen was the physiological age we brought them to in six months. Look for yourself what a splendid specimen it is. The reflexes are fifty percent above the human aged normally. The human musculature is beautifully engineered: a three-day-starved, six-month-atrophied myasthenia gravis case, can, with the proper stimulant drugs, overturn a ton and a half automobile. It will kill him—but that's still remarkable efficiency. Think what the biologically perfect body, operating, at all times at point nine-nine efficiency, could accomplish in physical strength alone."

"I thought hormone growth incentive had been outlawed. Doesn't it reduce the life span some drastic amount?"

"To the extent we used it, the life span reduction is seventy-five percent and over." He might have smiled the same way watching some odd animal at its incomprehensible antics. "But, Madam, we are making weapons. If TW-55 can function twenty years at peak efficiency, then it will have outlasted the average battle cruiser by five years. But the experiential imprinting! To find among ordinary men someone who can function as a spy, is *willing* to function as a spy, you must search the fringes of neurosis, often psychosis. Though such deviations might mean strength in a particular area, it always means an overall weakness in the personality. Functioning in any but that particular area, a spy may be dangerously inefficient. And the Invaders have psyche-indices too, which will keep the average spy out of any place we might want to put him. Captured, a good spy is a dozen times as dangerous as a bad one. Post-hypnotic suicide suggestions and the like are easily gotten around with drugs; and are wasteful. TW-55 here will register perfectly normal on a psyche integration. He has about six hours of social conversation, plot synopses of the latest novels, political situations, music, and art criticism—I believe in the course of an evening he is programmed to drop your name twice, an honor you share only with Ronald Quar. He has one subject on which he can expound with scholarly acumen for an hour and a half—this one is 'haptoglobin grouping among the marsupials,' I believe. Put him in formal wear and he will be perfectly at home at an ambassadorial ball or a coffee break at a high level government conference. He is a crack assassin, expert with all the weapons you have seen up till now, and more. TW-55 has twelve hours' worth of episodes in fourteen different dialects, accents, or jargons concerning sexual conquests, gambling experiences, fisticuff encounters, and humorous anecdotes of semi-illegal enterprises, all of which failed miserably. Tear his shirt, smear grease on his face and slip a pair of overalls on him, and he could be a service mechanic on any one of a hundred spaceyards or stellarcenters on the other side of the Snap. He can disable any space drive system, communications components, radar works, or alarm system used by the Invaders in the past twenty years with little more than——"

"Six inches of vanadium wire?"

The Baron smiled. "His fingerprints and retina pattern, he can alter at will. A little neural surgery has made all the muscles of his face voluntary, which means he can alter his facial structure drastically. Chemical dies and hormone banks beneath the scalp enable him to color his hair in seconds, or, if necessary, shed it completely and grow a new batch in half an hour. He's a past master in the psychology and physiology of coercion."

"Torture?"

"If you will. He is totally obedient to the people whom he has been conditioned to regard as his superiors; totally destructive toward what he has been ordered to destroy. There is nothing in that beautiful head even akin to a super-ego."

"He is ..." and she wondered at herself speaking, "beautiful." The dark lashed eyes with lids about to quiver open, the broad hands hung at the naked thighs, fingers half-curled, about to straighten or become a fist. The display light was misty on the tanned, yet near translucent skin. "You say this isn't a model, but really alive?"

"Oh, more or less. But it's rather firmly fixed in something like a yoga trance, or a lizard's hibernation. I could activate it for you—but it's ten to seven. We don't want to keep the others waiting at the table now, do we?"

She looked away from the figure in glass to the dull, taut skin of the Baron's face. His jaw, beneath his faintly concave cheek, was involuntarily working on its hinge.

"Like the circus," Rydra said. "But, I'm older now. Come." It was an act of will to offer her arm. His hand was paper dry, and so light she had to strain to keep from flinching.

IV

⁓⁓

"Captain Wong! I am delighted."

The Baroness extended her plump hand, of a pink and gray hue suggesting something parboiled. Her puffy freckled shoulders heaved beneath the straps of an evening dress tasteful enough over her distended figure, still grotesque.

"We have so little excitement here at the Yards that when someone as distinguished as yourself pays us a visit ..."

She let the sentence end in what would have been an ecstatic smile, but the weight of her doughy cheeks distorted it into a porcine pastiche of itself.

Rydra held the soft, malleable fingers as short a time as politeness allowed and returned the smile. She remembered, as a little girl, being obliged not to cry through punishment. Having the smile was worse. The Baroness seemed a muffled, vast, vacuous silence. The small muscle shifts, those counter communications that she was used to in direct conversation, were blunted in the Baroness under the fat. Even though the voice came from the heavy lips in strident little screeches, it was as though they talked through blankets.

"But your crew! We intended them all to be present. twenty-one, now I know that's what a full crew consists of." She shook her finger in patronizing disapproval. "I read up on these things, you know. And there are only eighteen of you here."

"I thought the discorporate members might remain on the ship," Rydra explained. "You need special equipment to talk with them and I thought they might upset your other guests. They're really more content with themselves for company and they don't eat."

They're having barbecued lamb for dinner and you'll go to hell for lying, she commented to herself—in Basque.

"Discorporate?" The Baroness patted the lacquered intricacies of her high-coifed hair. "You mean dead? Oh, of course. Now I hadn't thought of that at all. You see how cut off we are from one another in this world? I'll have their places removed." Rydra wondered whether the Baron had discorporate detecting equipment operating, as the Baroness leaned toward her and whispered confidentially, "Your crew has enchanted everybody! Shall we go on?"

With the Baron on her left—his palm a parchment sling for her forearm—and the Baroness leaning on her right—breathy and damp—they walked from the white stone foyer into the hall.

"Hey, Captain!" Calli bellowed, striding toward them from a quarter of the way across the room. "This is a pretty fine place, huh?" With his elbows he gestured around at the crowded hall, then held up his glass to show the size of his drink. He pursed his lips and nodded approvingly. "Let me get you some of these, Captain." Now he raised a handful of tiny sandwiches, olives stuffed with liver, and bacon-wrapped prunes. "There's a guy with a whole tray full running around over there." He pointed again with his elbow. "Ma'am, sir"—he looked from the Baroness to the Baron—"can I get you some, too?" He put one of the sandwiches in his mouth and followed it with a gulp from his glass. "Uhmpmnle."

"I'll wait till he brings them over here," the Baroness said.

Amused, Rydra glanced at her hostess, but there was a smile, much more the proper size, winding through her fleshy features. "I hope you like them."

Calli swallowed. "I do." Then he screwed up his face, set his teeth, opened his lips, and shook his head. *"Except* those real salty ones with the fish. I didn't like those at all, ma'am. But the rest are O.K."

"I'll tell you"—the Baroness leaned forward, the smile crumbling into a chesty chuckle—"I never really liked the salty ones either!"

She looked from Rydra to the Baron with a shrug of mock surrender. "But one is so tyrannized by one's caterer nowadays, what can one do?"

"If I didn't like them," Calli said, jerking his head aside in determination, "I'd tell him don't bring none!"

The Baronness looked back with raised eyebrows. "You know, you're perfectly right! That's exactly what I'm going to do!" She peered across Rydra to her husband. "That's just what I'm going to do, Felix, next time."

A waiter with a tray of glasses said, "Would you care for a drink?"

"She don't want one of them little tiny ones," Calli said, gesturing toward Rydra. "Get her a big one like I got."

Rydra laughed. "I'm afraid I have to be a lady tonight, Calli."

"Nonsense!" cried the Baroness. "I want a big one, too. Now let's see, I put the bar somewhere over there, didn't I?"

"That's where it was when I saw it last," Calli said.

"We're here to have fun this evening, and nobody is

going to have fun with one of *those*." She seized Rydra's arm and called back to her husband, "Felix, be sociable," and led Rydra away. "That's Dr. Keebling. The woman with the bleached hair is Dr. Crane, and that's my brother-in-law, Albert. I'll introduce you on the way back. They're all my husband's colleagues. They work with him on those dreadful things he was showing you in the cellar. I wish he wouldn't keep his private collection in the house. It's gruesome. I'm always afraid one of them will crawl up here in the middle of the night and chop our heads off. I think he's trying to make up for his son. You know we lost our little boy, Nyles—I think it's been eight years. Felix has thrown himself totally into his work since. But that's a terribly glib explanation, isn't it? Captain Wong, do you find us dreadfully provincial?"

"Not at all."

"You should. But then, you don't know any of us well, do you. Oh, the bright young people who come here, with their bright, lively imaginations. They do nothing all day long but think of ways to kill. It's a terribly placid society, really. But, why shouldn't it be? All its aggressions are vented from nine to five. Still, I think it does something to our minds. Imagination should be used for something other than pondering murder, don't you think?"

"I do." Concern grew for the weighty woman.

Just then they were stopped by clotted guests.

"What's going on here?" demanded the Baroness. "Sam, what are they doing in there?"

Sam smiled, stepped back, and the Baroness wedged herself into the space, still clutching Rydra's arm.

"Hold 'em back some!"

Rydra recognized Lizzy's voice. Someone else moved and she could see. The kids from Drive had cleared a space ten feet across, and were guarding it like junior police. Lizzy crouched with three boys, who, from their dress, were local gentry of Armsedge. "What you have to understand," she was saying, "is that it's all in the wrist." She flipped a marble with her thumbnail: it struck first one, then another, and one of the struck ones struck a third.

"Hey, do that again!"

Lizzy picked up another marble. "Only one knuckle on

the floor, now, so you can pivot. But it's mostly from the wrist.''

The marble darted out, struck, struck, and struck. Five or six people applauded. Rydra was one.

The Baroness touched her breast. "Lovely shot! Perfectly lovely!'' She remembered herself and glanced back. "Oh, you must want to watch this, Sam. You're the ballistics expert, anyway.'' With polite embarrassment she relinquished her place and turned to Rydra as they continued across the floor. "There. There, that is why I'm so glad you and your crew came to see us this evening. You bring something so cool and pleasing, so fresh, so crisp.''

"You speak about us as though we were a salad.'' Rydra laughed. In the Baroness the ''appetite' was not so menacing.

"I dare say if you stayed here long enough we would devour you, if you let us. What you bring we are very hungry for.''

"What is it?''

They arrived at the bar, then turned with their drinks. The Baroness' face strained toward hardness. "Well, you . . . you come to us and immediately we start to learn things, things about you, and ultimately about ourselves.''

"I don't understand.''

"Take your Navigator. He likes his drinks big and all the hors d'oeuvres except the anchovies. That's more than I know about the likes and dislikes of anyone else in the room. You offer Scotch, they drink Scotch. You offer tequila, tequila they then down by the gallon. And just a moment ago I discovered''—she shook her supine hand—''that it's all in the wrist. I never knew *that* before.''

"We're used to talking to each other.''

"Yes, but you tell the important things. What you like, what you don't like, how you do things. Do you really want to be introduced to all those stuffy men and women who kill people?''

"Not really.''

"Didn't think so. And I don't want to bother myself. Oh, there are three or four who I think you would like. But I'll see that you meet them before you leave.'' She barreled into the crowd.

Tides, Rydra thought. Oceans. Hyperstasis currents. Or the movement of people in a large room. She drifted along the least resistant ways that pulsed open, then closed as someone moved to meet someone, to get a drink, to leave a conversation.

Then there was a corner, a spiral stair. She climbed, pausing as she came around the second turn to watch the crowd beneath. There was a double door ajar at the top, a breeze. She stepped outside.

Violet had been replaced by artful, cloud-streaked purple. Soon the planetoid's chromadome would simulate night. Moist vegetation lipped the railing. At one end, the vines had completely covered the white stone.

"Captain?"

Ron, shadowed and brushed with leaves, sat in the corner of the balcony, hugging his knees. Skin is not silver, she thought, yet whenever I see him that way, curled up in himself, I picture a knot of white metal. He lifted his chin from his kneecaps and put his back against the verdant hedge so there were leaves in his corn-silk hair.

"What're you doing?"

"Too many people."

She nodded, watching him press his shoulders downward, watching his triceps leap on the bone, then still. With each breath in the young, gnarled body the tiny movements sang to her. She listened to the singing for nearly half a minute while he watched her, sitting still, yet always the tiny entrancements. The rose on his shoulder whispered against the leaves. When she had listened to the muscular music a while, she asked:

"Trouble between you, Mollya, and Calli?"

"No. I mean . . . just . . ."

"Just what?" She smiled and leaned on the balcony edge.

He lowered his chin to his knees again. "I guess they're fine. But, I'm the youngest . . . and . . ." Suddenly the shoulders raised. "How the hell would you understand! Sure, you know about things like this, but you don't really know. You write what you see. Not what you do." It came out in little explosions of half whispered sound. She heard the words and watched the jaw muscle jerk and beat and pop, a small beast inside his cheek. "Perverts," he said. "That's what you Customs all really think. The Baron and the Baroness, all those people in there staring at us, who can't understand why you could want more than two. And you can't understand either."

"Ron?"

He snapped his teeth on a leaf and yanked it from the stem.

"Five years ago, Ron, I was . . . tripled."

The face turned to her as if pulling against a spring, then yanked back. He spit the leaf. "You're Customs, Captain. You circle Transport, but just the way you let them eat you up with their eyes, the way they turn and watch to see who you are when you walk by: you're a Queen, yeah. But a Queen in Customs. You're not Transport."

"Ron, I'm public. That's why they look. I write books. Customs people read them, yes, but they look because they want to know who the hell wrote them. Customs didn't write them. I talk to Customs and Customs looks at me and says: 'You're Transport.' " She shrugged. "I'm neither. But even so, I was tripled. I know about that."

"Customs don't triple," he said.

"Two guys and myself. If I ever do it again it'll be with a girl and a guy. For me that would be easier, I think. But I was tripled for three years. That's over twice as long as you've been."

"Yours didn't stick, then. Ours did. At least it was sticking together with Cathy."

"One was killed," Rydra said. "One is in suspended animation at Hippocrates General waiting for them to discover a cure for Caulder's disease. I don't think it will be in my lifetime, but if it is——" In the silence he turned to her. "What is it?" she asked.

"Who were they?"

"Customs or Transport?" She shrugged. "Like me, neither really. Fobo Lombs, he was captain of an interstellar transport; he was the one who made me go through and get my Captain's papers. Also he worked planetside doing hydroponics research, working on storage methods for hyperstatic hauls. Who was he? He was slim and blond and wonderfully affectionate and drank too much sometimes, and would come back from a trip and get drunk and in a fight and in jail, and we'd bail him out—really it only happened twice—but we teased him with it for a year. And he didn't like to sleep in the middle of the bed because he always wanted to let one arm hang over.''

Ron laughed, and his hands, grasping high on his forearms, slid to his wrists.

''He was killed in a cave-in exploring the Ganymede Catacombs during the second summer that the three of us worked together on the Jovian Geological Survey.''

''Like Cathy,'' Ron said, after a moment.

''Muels Aranlyde was——''

''*Empire Star!*'' Ron said, his eyes widening, ''and the 'Comet Jo' books! You were tripled with Muels Aranlyde?''

She nodded. ''Those books were a lot of fun, weren't they?''

''Hell, I must've read all of them,'' Ron said. His knees came apart. ''What sort of a guy was he? Was he anything like Comet?''

''As a matter of fact, Comet Jo started out to be Fobo. Fobo would get involved in something or other, I'd get upset, and Muels would start another novel.''

''You mean they're like true stories?''

She shook her head. ''Most of the books are just all the fantastic things that could have happened, or that we worried might have happened. Muels himself? In the books he always disguises himself as a computer. He was dark, and withdrawn, and incredibly patient and incredibly kind. He showed me all about sentences and paragraphs—did you know the emotional unit in writing is the paragraph?—and how to separate what you can say from what you can imply, and when to do one or the other——'' She stopped. ''Then he'd give me a manuscript and say, 'Now you tell me what's wrong with the words.' The only thing I could ever find was that there were too many of them. It was just after Fobo was killed that I really got down to my poetry. Muels used to tell me if I ever would, I'd be great because I knew so much about its elements to start. I had to get down something then, because Fobo was...but you know about that, though. Muels caught Caulder's disease about four months later. Neither one of them saw my first book, though they'd seen most of the poems. Maybe someday Muels will read them. He might even write some more of Comet's adventures—and maybe even go to the Morgue and call back my thinking pattern and ask, 'Now tell me what's wrong with the words'; and I'll be able to tell him so much more, so much. But there won't be any consciousness left..." She felt herself drift toward the dangerous emotions, let them get as close as they would. Dangerous or not, it had been three years since her emotions had scared her too much to watch them. "...so much more."

Ron sat cross-legged now, forearms on his knees, hands hanging.

"*Empire Star* and Comet Jo; we had so much fun with those stories, whether it was arguing about them all night over coffee, or correcting galleys, or sneaking into bookshops and pulling them out from behind the other books."

"I used to do that, too," Ron said. "But just 'cause I liked them."

"We even had fun arguing about who was going to sleep in the middle."

It was like a cue. Ron began to pull back together, knees rising, arms locking around them, chin down. "I got both of mine, at least," he said. "I guess I should be pretty happy."

"Maybe you should. Maybe you shouldn't. Do they love you?"

"They said so."

"Do you love them?"

"Christ, yes. I talk to Mollya and she's trying to explain something to me and she still don't talk so good yet, but suddenly I figure out what she means, and..." He straightened his body and looked up as though the word he was searching for was someplace high.

"It's wonderful," she supplied.

"Yeah, it's——" He looked at her. "It's wonderful."

"You and Calli?"

"Hell, Calli's just a big old bear and I can tumble him around and play with him. But it's him and Mollya. He still can't understand her so well. And because I'm the youngest, he thinks he should learn quicker than me. And he doesn't, so he keeps away from both of us. Now like I say, when he gets in a mood, I can always handle him. But she's new, and thinks he's mad at her."

"Want to know what to do?" Rydra asked, after a moment.

"Do you know?"

She nodded. "It hurts more when there's something wrong between them because there doesn't seem to be anything you can do. But it's easier to fix."

"Why?"

"Because they love you."

He was waiting now.

"Calli gets into one of his moods, and Mollya doesn't know how to get through to him."

Ron nodded.

"Mollya speaks another language, and Calli can't get through that."

He nodded again.

"Now you can communicate with both of them. You can't act as a go-between; that never works. But you can teach each of them how to do what you know already."

"Teach?"

"What do you do with Calli when he gets moody?"

"I pull his ears," Ron said. "He tells me to cut it out until he starts laughing, and then I roll him around on the floor."

Rydra made a face. "It's unorthodox, but if it works, fine. Now show Mollya how. She's athletic. Let her practice on you till she gets it right, if you have to."

"I don't like to get *my* ears pulled," Ron said.

"Sometimes you have to make sacrifices." She tried not to smile; and smiled anyway.

Ron rubbed his left earlobe with the ham of his thumb. "I guess so."

"And you have to teach Calli the words to get through to Mollya."

"But I don't know the words myself, sometimes. I can just guess better than he can."

"If he knew the words, would it help?"

"Sure."

"I've got Kiswahili grammar books in my cabin. Pick them up when we get back to the ship."

"Hey, that would be fine——" He stopped, withdrawing just a bit into the leaves. "Only Calli don't read much or anything."

"You'll help him."

"Teach him," Ron said.

"That's right."

"Do you think he'll do it?" Ron asked.

"To get closer to Mollya?" asked Rydra. "Do you think so?"

"He will." Like metal unbending, Ron suddenly stood. "He will."

"Are you going inside now?" she asked. "We'll be eating in a few minutes."

Ron turned to the rail and looked at the vivid sky. "They keep a beautiful shield up here."

"To keep from being burned up by Bellatrix," Rydra said.

"So they don't have to think about what they're doing."

Rydra raised her eyebrows. Still the concern over right and wrong, even amidst domestic confusion. "That, too," she said and wondered about the war.

His tensing back told her he would come later, wanted to think some more. She went through the double doors and started down the staircase.

"I saw you go out, and I thought I'd wait for you to come back in."

Déja vu, she thought. But she couldn't have seen him before in her life. Blue-black hair over a face craggy for its age in the late twenties. He stepped back to make way for her on the stairway with an incredible economy of movement. She looked from hands to face for a gesture revealing something. He watched her back, giving nothing; then he turned and nodded toward the people below. He indicated the Baron, who stood alone toward the middle of the room. "Yon Cassius has a lean and hungry look."

"I wonder how hungry he is?" Rydra said, and felt strange again.

The Baroness was churning toward her husband through the crowd, to ask advice about whether to begin dinner or wait another five minutes, or some other equally desperate decision.

"What must a marriage between two people like that be?" the stranger asked with austerely patronizing amusement.

"Comparatively simple, I suppose," Rydra said. "They've just got each other to worry about."

A polite look of inquiry. When she offered no elucidation, the stranger turned back to the crowd. "They make such odd faces when they glance up here to see if it's you, Miss Wong."

"They leer," she said, shortly.

"Bandicoots. That's what they look like. A pack of them."

"I wonder if their artificial sky makes them seem so sickly?" She felt herself leaking a controlled hostility.

He laughed. "Bandicoots with thalassanemia!"

"I guess so. You're not from the Yards?" His complexion had a life that would have faded under the artificial sky.

"As a matter of fact, I am."

Surprised, she would have asked him more, but the loudspeakers suddenly announced: "Ladies and Gentlemen, dinner is served."

He accompanied her down the stairs, but two or three steps into the crowd she discovered he had disappeared. She continued toward the dining room alone.

Under the arch the Baron and Baroness waited for her. As the Baroness took her arm, the chamber orchestra on the dais fell to their instruments.

"Come, we're down this way."

She kept near the puffy matron through the people milling about the serpentine table that curved and twisted back on itself.

"We're over there."

And the Basque message: Captain, on your transcriber,

something's coming over back on the ship. The small explosion in her mind stopped her.

"Babel-17!"

The Baron turned to her. "Yes, Captain Wong?" She watched uncertainty score tense lines on his face.

"Is there any place in the yards with particularly important materials or research going on that might be unguarded now?"

"That's all done automatically. Why?"

"Baron, there's a sabotage attack about to take place, or taking place right now."

"But how did you——"

"I can't explain now, but you'd better make sure everything is all right."

And the tension turned.

The Baroness touched her husband's arm, and said with sudden coolness. "Felix, there's your seat."

The Baron pulled out his chair, sat down, and unceremoniously pushed aside his place setting. There was a control panel beneath the doily. As people seated themselves, Rydra saw Brass, twenty feet away, lower himself on the special hammock that had been set up for his glittering, gigantic bulk.

"You sit here, my dear. We'll simply go on with the party as if nothing was happening. I think that's best."

Rydra seated herself next to the Baron, and the Baroness lowered herself carefully to the chair on her left. The Baron was whispering into a throat microphone. Pictures, which she was at the wrong angle to see clearly, flashed on the eight inch screen. He looked up long enough to say, "Nothing yet, Captain Wong."

"Ignore what he's doing," the Baroness said. "This is much more interesting over here."

Into her lap she swung out a small console from where it had hung beneath the table edge.

"Ingenious little thing," the Baroness continued, looking around. "I think we're ready. There!" Her pudgy forefinger struck at one of the buttons, and lights about the room began to lower. "I control the whole meal just by pressing the right one at the right time. Watch!'' She struck at another one.

Along the center of the table now, under the gentled light, panels opened and great platters of fruit, candied apples and sugared grapes, halved melons filled with honeyed nuts, rose up before the guests.

''And wine!'' said the Baroness, reaching down again.

Along the hundreds of feet of table, basins rose. Sparkling froth foamed the brim as the fountain mechanism began. Spurting liquid streamed.

''Fill your glass, dear. Drink up,'' prompted the Baroness, raising her own beneath a jet; the crystal splashed with purple.

On her right the Baron said: ''The Arsenal seems to be all right. I'm alerting all the special projects. You're sure this sabotage attack is going on right now?''

''Either right now,'' she told him, ''or within the next two or three minutes. It might be an explosion, or some major piece of equipment may fail.''

''That doesn't leave me much to go on. Though communications has picked up your Babel-17. I've been alerted to how these attempts run.''

''Try one of these, Captain Wong.'' The Baroness handed her a quartered mango which Rydra discovered, when she tasted it, had been marinated in Kirsch.

Nearly all the guests were seated now. She watched a platoon kid, named Mike, searching for his name-card halfway across the hall. And down the table length she saw the stranger who had stopped her on the spiral stair hurrying toward them behind the seated guests.

''The wine is not grape, but plum,'' the Baroness said. ''A little heavy to start with, but so good with fruit. I'm particularly proud of the strawberries. The legumes are a hydroponicist's nightmare, you know, but this year we were able to get such lovely ones.''

Mike found his seat and reached both hands into the fruit bowl. The stranger rounded the last loop of table. Calli was holding a goblet of wine in each hand, looking from one to the other, trying to determine the larger.

''I could be a tease,'' the Baroness said, ''and bring out

the sherbets first. Or do you think I ought best go on to the caldo verde? The way I prepare it, it's very light. I can never decide——''

The stranger reached the Baron, leaned over his shoulder to watch the screen, and whispered something. The Baron turned to him, turned back slowly with both hands on the table—and fell forward! A trickle of blood wormed from beneath his face.

Rydra jerked back in her chair. Murder. A mosaic came together in her head, and when it was together, it said: murder. She leapt up.

The Baroness exhaled hoarse breath and rose, overturning her chair. She flapped her hands hysterically toward her husband and shook her head.

Rydra whirled to see the stranger snatch a vibra-gun from beneath his jacket. She yanked the Baroness out of the way. The shot was low and struck the console.

Once moved, the Baroness staggered to her husband and grasped him. Her breathy moan took voice and became a wail. The hulking form, like a blimp deflating, sank and pulled Felix Ver Dorco's body from the table, till she was kneeling on the floor, holding him in her arms, rocking him gently, screaming.

Guests had risen now; talking became roaring.

With the console smashed, along the table the fruit platters were pushed aside by emerging peacocks, cooked, dressed, and reassembled with sugared heads, tail feathers swaying. None of the clearing mechanisms were operating. Tureens of caldo verde crowded the wine basins till both overturned, flooding the table. Fruit rolled over the edge.

Through the voices, the vibra-gun hissed on her left, left again, then right. People ran from their chairs, blocked her view. She heard the gun once more and saw Dr. Crane double over, to be caught by a surprised neighbor as her bleached hair came undone and tumbled her face.

Spitted lambs rose to upset the peacocks. Feathers swept the floor. Wine fountains spurted the glistening amber skins which hissed and steamed. Food fell back into the opening and struck red heating coils. Rydra smelled burning.

She darted forward, caught the arm of the fat, black-bearded man. "Slug, get the kids out of here!"

"What do you think I'm doing, Captain?"

She darted away, came up against a length of table, and vaulted the steaming pit. The intricate, oriental dessert—sizzling bananas dipped first in honey then rolled to the plate over a ramp of crushed ice—was emerging as she sprang. The sparkling confections shot across the ramp and dropped to the floor, honey crystallized to glittering thorns. They rolled among the guests, cracked underfoot. People slipped and flailed and fell.

"Snazzy way to slide on a banana, huh, Captain?" commented Calli. "What's going on?"

"Get Mollya and Ron back to the ship!"

Urns rose now, struck the rotisserie arrangement, overturned, and grounds and boiling coffee splattered. A woman shrieked, clutching her scalded arm.

"This ain't no fun anymore," Calli said. "I'll round them up."

He started away as Slug hurried back the other way. "Slug, what's a bandicoot?" She caught his arm again.

"Vicious little animal. Marsupial, I think. Why?"

"That's right. I remember now. And thalassanemia?"

"Funny time to ask. Some sort of anemia."

"I know that. *What* sort? You're the medic on the ship."

"Let me see." He closed his eyes a moment. "I got all this once in a hypno-course. Yeah, I remember. It's hereditary, the Caucasian equivalent of sickle cell anemia, where the red blood cells collapse because the haptoglobins break down——"

"—and allow the hemoglobins to leak out and the cell gets crushed by osmotic pressure. I've figured it out. Get the hell out of here."

Puzzled, the Slug started toward the arch.

Rydra started after him, slipped in wine sherbet, and grabbed Brass, who now gleamed above her. "Take it easy, Ca'tain!"

"Out of here, baby," she demanded. "And fast."

"Ho' a ride?" Grinning, he hooked his arms at his hip, and she climbed to his back, clutching his sides with her knees and holding his shoulders. The great muscles that had defeated the Silver Dragon bunched beneath her, and he leapt, clearing the table and landing on all fours. Before the fanged, golden beast, guests scattered. They made for the arched door.

V

~~~~~~

Hysterical exhaustion frothed.

She smashed through it, into the *Rimbaud*'s cabin, and punched the intercom. "Slug, is every——"

"All present and accounted for, Captain,"

"The discorporate——"

"Safe aboard, all three."

Brass, panting, filled the entrance hatch behind her.

She switched to another channel, and a near musical sound filled the room. "Good. It's still going."

"That's it?" asked Brass.

She nodded. "Babel-17. It's been automatically transcribed so I can study it later. Anyway, here goes nothing." She threw a switch.

"What you doing?"

"I prerecorded some messages and I'm sending them out now. Maybe they'll get through." She stopped the first take and started a second. "I don't know it well, yet. I know a little, but not enough. I feel like someone at a performance of Shakespeare shouting catcalls in pidgin English."

An outside line signaled for her attention. "Captain Wong, this is Albert Ver Dorco." The voice was perturbed. "We've had a terrible catastrophe, and we're in total confusion here. I could not find you at my brother's, but flight clearance just told me you had requested immediate take off for hyperstasis jump."

"I requested nothing of the kind. I just wanted to get my

crew out of there. Have you found out what's going on?''

"But, Captain, they said you were in the process of clearing for flight. You have top priority, so I can't very well countermand your order. But I called to request that you please stay until this matter is cleared up, unless you are acting on some imformation that——''

"We're not taking off," Rydra said.

"We better not be," interjected Brass. "I'm not wired into the ship yet."

"Apparently your automatic James Bond ran berserk," Rydra told Ver Dorco.

". . . Bond?"

"A mythological reference. Forgive me. TW-55 flipped."

"Oh, yes. I know. It assassinated my brother, and four extremely important officials. It couldn't have picked out four more key figures if it had been planned."

"It was. TW-55 was sabotaged. And no, I don't know how. I suggest you contact General Forester back at——''

"Captain, flight clearance says you're still signaling for take off! I have no official authority here, but you must——''

"Slug! Are we taking off?"

"Why, yes. Didn't you just issue orders down here for emergency hyperstasis exit?"

"Brass isn't even at his station yet, you idiot!"

"But I just received clearance from you thirty seconds ago. Of course he's hooked in. I just spoke——''

Brass lumbered across the floor and bellowed into the microphone. "I'm standing right behind her, numbskull! What are you gonna do, dive into the middle of Bellatrix? Or maybe come out inside some nova? These things head for the biggest mass around when they drift!"

"But you just——''

A grinding started somewhere below them. And a sudden surge.

Over the loudspeaker from Albert Ver Dorco: "Captain Wong!"

Rydra shouted again, "Idiot, cut the stasis gen——''

But the generators were already whistling over the roar.

And surge again; she jerked against her hands holding the desk edge, saw Brass flail one claw in the air. And—

PART THREE

~~~~~~

Jebel Tarik

Real, grimy, and exiled, he
eludes us.
I would show him books and bridges.
I would make a language we could all speak.
No blond fantasy
Mother has sent to plague us in the Spring,
he has his own bad dreams, needs work, gets drunk,
maybe would not have chosen to be beautiful.

—from *The Navigators*

You have imposed upon me a treaty of silence.

—from *The Song of Liadan*

1

~~~~~~

Abstract thoughts in a blue room: Nominative, genitive, elative, accusative one, accusative two, ablative, partitive, illative, instructive, abessive, adessive, inessive, essive, allative, translative, comitative. Sixteen cases to the Finnish noun. Odd, some languages get by with only singular and plural. The North American Indian languages even failed to distinguish number. Except Sioux, in which there was a plural only for animate objects. The blue room was round and warm and smooth. No way to say *warm* in French. There was only *hot* and *tepid*. If there's no word for it, how do you think about it? And, if there isn't the proper form, you don't have the how even if you have the words. Imagine, in Spanish having to assign a gender to every object: dog, table, tree, can-opener. Imagine, in Hungarian, not being able to assign a gender to anything: *he, she, it* all the same word. Thou art my friend, but you are my king; thus the distinctions of Elizabeth the First's English. But with some oriental languages, which all but dispense with gender and number, you are my friend, *you* are my parent, and YOU are my priest, and *YOU* are my king, and **You** are my servant, and *You* are my servant whom I'm going to fire tomorrow if *You* don't watch it, and YOU are my king whose policies I totally disagree with and have sawdust in **YOUR** head instead of brains, **YOUR** highness, and YOU may be my friend, but I'm still gonna smack YOU up side the head if YOU ever say that to me again: and who the hell are you anyway . . . ?

What's your name? she thought in a round warm blue room.

Thoughts without a name in a blue room: Ursula, Priscilla, Barbara, Mary, Mona, and Natica: respectively, Bear, Old Lady, Chatterbox, Bitter, Monkey, and Buttock. Name. Names? What's in a name? What name am I in? In my father's father's land, his name would come first, Wong Rydra. In Mollya's home, I would not bear my father's name at all, but my mother's. Words are names for things. In Plato's time things were names for ideas—what better description of the Platonic Ideal? But were words names for things, or was that just a bit of semantic confusion? Words were symbols for *whole* categories of things, where a name was put to a single object: a name on something that requires a symbol jars, making humor. A symbol on something that takes a name jars, too: a memory that contained a torn window shade, his liquored breath, her outrage, and crumpled clothing wedged behind a chipped, cheap night table, "All right, *woman*, come here!" and she had whispered, with her hands achingly tight on the brass bar, "My *name* is *Rydra!*" An individual, a thing apart from its environment, and apart from all things in that environment; an individual was a type of thing for which symbols were inadequate, and so names were invented. I am invented. I am not a round warm blue room. I am someone in that room, I am—

Her lids had been half-closed on her eyeballs. She opened them and came up suddenly against a restraining web. It knocked her breath out, and she fell back, turning about to look at the room.

No.

She didn't "look at the room."

She "*something*ed at the *something*." The first something was a tiny vocable that implied an immediate, but passive, perception that could be aural or olfactory as well as visual. The second something was three equally tiny phonemes that blended at different musical pitches: one, an indicator that fixed the size of the chamber at roughly twenty-five feet cubical, the second identifying the color and probable substance of the walls—some blue metal—while the third was at once a place holder for particles that should denote the room's function when she discovered it, and a sort of grammatical tag by which she could refer to the whole experience with only the one symbol for as long as she needed. All four sounds took less time on her tongue and in her mind than the one clumsy diphthong in *'room'*. Babel-17; she had felt it before with other languages, the opening, the widening, the mind forced to sudden growth. But this, this was like the sudden focusing of a lens blurry for years.

She sat up again. Function?

What was the room used for? She rose slowly, and the web caught her around the chest. Some sort of infirmary. She looked down at the—not 'webbing', but rather a three particle vowel differential, each particle of which defined one stress of the three-way tie, so that the weakest points in the mesh were identified when the total sound of the differential reached its lowest point. By breaking the threads at these points, she realized, the whole web would unravel. Had she flailed at it, and not named it in this new language, it would have been more than secure enough to hold her. The transition from 'memorized' to 'known' had taken place while she had been——

Where had she been? Anticipation, excitement, fear! She pulled her mind back into English. Thinking in Babel-17 was like suddenly seeing through water at the bottom of a well that a moment ago you thought had only gone down a few feet. She reeled with vertigo.

It took her a blink to register the others. Brass hung in the large hammock at the far wall—she saw the tines of one yellow claw over the rim. The two smaller hammocks on the other side must have been platoon kids. Above one edge she saw shiny black hair as a head turned in sleep: Carlos. She couldn't see the third. Curiosity made a small, unfriendly fist on something important in her lower abdomen.

Then the wall faded.

She had been about to try and fix herself, if not in place and hour, at least in some set of possibilities. With the fading wall, the attempt stopped. She watched.

It happened in the upper part of the wall to her left. It glowed, grew transparent, and a tongue of metal formed in the air, sloped gently toward her.

Three men:

The closest, at the ramp's head, had a face like brown

rock cut roughly and put together fast. He wore an outdated garment, the sort that had preceded contour capes. It automatically formed to the body, but was made of porous plastic and looked rather like armor. A black, deep piled material cloaked one shoulder and arm. His worn sandals were laced high on his calves. Tufts of fur beneath the thongs prevented chafing. His only cosmetisurgery was false silver hair and upswept metallic eyebrows. From one distended earlobe hung a thick silver ring. He touched his vibra-gun holster resting on his stomach as he looked from hammock to hammock.

The second man stepped in front. He was a slim, fantastic concoction of cosmetisurgical invention, sort of a griffin, sort of a monkey, sort of a sea horse: scales, feathers, claws, and beak had been grafted to a body she was sure had originally resembled a cat's. He crouched at the first man's side, squatting on surgically distended haunches, brushing his knuckles on the metal flooring. He glanced up as the first man absently reached down to scratch his head.

Rydra waited for them to speak. A word would release identification: Alliance or Invader. Her mind was ready to spring on whatever tongue they spoke, to extract what she knew of its thinking habits, tendencies toward logical ambiguities, absence or presence of verbal rigor, in whatever areas she might take advantage of—

The second man moved back and she saw the third who still stood at the rear. Taller, and more powerfully built than the others, he wore only a breech, was mildly round-shouldered. Grafted onto his wrists and heels were cocks' spurs—they were sometimes sported by the lower elements of the transport underworld, and bore the same significance as brass knuckles or blackjacks of centuries past. His head had been recently shaved and the hair had started back in a dark, Elektra brush. Around one knotty bicep was a band of red flesh, like a blood bruise or inflamed scar. The brand had become so common on characters in mystery novels five years back that now it had been nearly dropped as a hopeless cliché. It was a convict's mark from the penal caves of Titin. Something about him was brutal enough to make her glance away. Something was graceful enough to make her look back.

The two on the head of the ramp turned to the third. She

waited for words, to define, fix, identify. They looked at her, then walked into the wall. The ramp began to retract.

She pushed herself up. "Please," she called out. "Where are we?"

The silver-haired man said, "Jebel Tarik." The wall solidified.

Rydra looked down at the web (which was something else in another language) popped one cord, popped another. The tension gave, till it unraveled and she jumped to the floor. As she stood she saw the other platoon kid was Kile, who worked with Lizzy in Repair. Brass had started struggling. "Keep still a second." She began to pop cords.

"What did he say to you?" Brass wanted to know. "Was that his name, or was he telling you to lie down and shut u'?"

She shrugged and broke another. "Jebel, that's *mountain* in Old Moorish. Tarik's Mountain, maybe."

Brass sat up as the frayed string fell. "How do you do that?" he asked. "I pushed against the thing for ten minutes and it wouldn't give."

"Tell you some other time. Tarik could be somebody's name."

Brass looked back at the broken web, clawed behind one tufted ear, then shook his puzzled head and reared.

"At least they're not Invaders," Rydra said.

"Who says?"

"I doubt that many humans on the other side of the axis have even heard of Old Moorish. The Earthmen who migrated there all came from North and South America before Americasia was formed and Pan Africa swallowed up Europe. Besides, the Titin penal caves are inside Caesar."

"Oh yea," Brass said. "Him. But that don't mean one of its alumni has to be."

She looked at where the wall had opened. Grasping their situation seemed as futile as grasping that blue metal.

"What the hell ha''ened anyway?"

"We took off without a pilot," Rydra said. "I guess whoever broadcast in Babel-17 can also broadcast English."

"I don't think we took off without a 'ilot. Who did Slug talk to just before we shot? If we didn't have a 'ilot, we wouldn't be here. We'd be a grease s'ot on the nearest, biggest sun.''

"Probably whoever cracked those circuit boards." Rydra cast her mind into the past as the plaster of unconsciousness crumbled. "I guess the saboteur doesn't want to kill me. TW-55 could have picked me off as easily as he picked off the Baron.''

"I wonder if the s'y on the shi' s'eaks Babel-17 too?''

Rydra nodded. "So do I.''

Brass looked around. "Is this all there is? Where's the rest of the crew?''

"Sir, Ma'am?''

They turned.

Another opening in the wall. A skinny girl, with a green scarf binding back brown hair, held out a bowl.

"The master said you were about, so I brought this." Her eyes were dark and large, and the lids beat like bird wings. She gestured with the bowl.

Rydra responded to her openness, yet also detected a fear of strangers. But the thin fingers grasped surely on the bowl's edge. "You're kind to bring this.''

The girl bowed slightly and smiled.

"You're frightened of us, I know," Rydra said. "You shouldn't be.''

The fear was leaving; bony shoulders relaxed.

"What's your master's name?" Rydra asked.

"Tarik.''

Rydra looked back and nodded to Brass.

"And we're in Tarik's Mountain?" She took the bowl from the girl. "How did we get here?''

"He hooked your ship up from the center of the Cygnus-42 nova just before your stasis generators failed this side of the jump.''

Brass hissed, his substitute for a whistle. "No wonder we went unconscious. We did some fast drifting.''

The thought pulled the plug from Rydra's stomach. "Then we did drift into a nova area. Maybe we didn't have a pilot after all.''

Brass removed the white napkin from the bowl. "Have some chicken, Ca'tain." It was roasted and still hot.

"In a minute," she said. "I have to think about that one some more." She turned back to the girl. "Tarik's Mountain is a ship, then. And we're on it?"

The girl put her hands behind her back and nodded. "And it's a good ship, too."

"I'm sure you don't take passengers. What cargo do you haul?"

She had asked the wrong question. Fear again; not a personal distrust of strangers, something formal and pervasive. "We carry no cargo, ma'am." Then she blurted, "I'm not supposed to talk to you none. You have to speak with Tarik." She backed into the wall.

"Brass," Rydra said, turning and scratching her head, "there're no space-pirates any more, are there?"

"There haven't been any hi-jacks on transport ships for seventy years."

"That's what I thought. So what sort of ship are we on?"

"Beats me." Then the burnished planes of his cheeks shifted in the blue light. Silken brows pulled down over the deep disks of his eyes. *"Hooked* the *Rimbaud* out of the Cygnus-42? I guess I know why they call it Tarik's Mountain. This thing must be big as a damn battleshi'."

"If it is a warship, Tarik doesn't look like any stellarman I ever saw."

"And they don't allow ex-convicts in the army, anyway. What do you think we've stumbled on, Ca'tain?"

She took a drumstick from the bowl. "I guess we wait till we speak to Tarik." There was movement in the other hammocks. "I hope the kids are all right. Why didn't I ask that girl if the rest of the crew was aboard?" She strode to Carlos' hammock. "How do *you* feel this morning?" she asked brightly. For the first time she saw the snaps that held the webbing to the underside of the sling.

"My head," Carlos said, grinning. "I got a hangover, I think."

"Not with that leer on your face. What do you know about hangovers, anyway?" The snaps took three times as long to undo as breaking the net.

"The wine," Carlos said, "at the party. I had a lot. Hey, what happened?"

"Tell you when I find out. Upsy-daisy." She tipped the hammock and he rolled to his feet.

Carlos pushed the hair out of his eyes. "Where's everybody else?"

"Kile's over there. That's all of us in this room."

Brass had freed Kile, who sat on the hammock edge now, trying to put his knuckles up his nose.

"Hey, baby," Carlos said. "You all right?"

Kile ran his toes up and down his Achilles tendon, yawned, and said something unintelligible at the same time.

"You did not," Carlos said, "because I checked it just as soon as I got in."

Oh well, she thought, there were still languages left at which she might gain more fluency.

Kile was scratching his elbow now. Suddenly he stuck his tongue in the corner of his mouth and looked up.

So did Rydra.

The ramp was extending from the wall again. This time it joined the floor.

"Will you come with me, Rydra Wong?"

Tarik, holstered and silver-haired, stood in the dark opening.

"The rest of my crew," Rydra said, "are they all right?"

"They are all in other wards. If you wish to see them——"

"Are they all right?"

Tarik nodded.

Rydra thumped Carlos on his head. "I'll see you later," she whispered.

The commons was arched and balconied, the walls dull as rock. The expanses were hung with green and crimson zodiac signs or representations of battles. And the stars—at first, she thought the light flecked void beyond the gallery columns was an actual view-port; but it was only a great hundred-foot long projection of the night beyond their ship.

Men and women sat and talked around wooden tables, or lounged by the walls. Down a broad set of steps was a wide counter filled with food and pitchers. The opening hung with pots, pans, and platters, and behind it she saw the aluminium and white recess of the galley where aproned men and women prepared dinner.

The company turned when they entered. Those nearest touched their foreheads in salute. She followed Tarik to the raised steps and walked to the cushioned benches at the top.

The griffin man came scurrying up. "Master, this is she?" Tarik turned to Rydra, his rocky face softening. "This is my amusement, my distraction, my ease of ire, Captain Wong. In him I keep the sense of humor that all around will tell you I lack. Hey, Klik, leap up and straighten the seats for conference."

The feathered head ducked brightly, black eye winking, and Klik whacked the cushions puffy. A moment later Tarik and Rydra sank into them.

"Tarik," asked Rydra, "what route does your ship run?"

"We stay in the Specelli Snap." He pushed his cape back from his three-knobbed shoulder. "What was your original position before you were caught up in the noval tide?"

"We . . . took off from the War Yards at Armsedge."

Tarik nodded. "You are fortunate. Most shadow-ships would have left you to emerge in the nova when your generators gave out. It would have been a rather final discorporation."

"I guess so." Rydra felt her stomach sink at the memory. Then she asked, "Shadow-ships?"

"Yes. That's Jebel Tarik."

"I'm afraid I don't know what a shadow-ship is."

Tarik laughed, a soft, rough sound in the back of his throat. "Perhaps it's just as well. I hope you never have occasion to wish I had not told you."

"Go ahead," Rydra said. "I'm listening."

"The Specelli Snap is radio-dense. A ship, even a mountain like Tarik, over any long-range is undetectable. It also runs across the stasis side of Cancer."

"That galaxy lies under the Invaders," Rydra said, with conditioned apprehension.

"The Snap is the boundary along Cancer's edge. We . . .

patrol the area and keep the Invader ships . . . in their place.''

Rydra watched the hesitation in his face. "But not officially?''

Again he laughed. "How could we, Captain Wong?'' He stroked a ruff of feathers between Klik's shoulder blades. The jester arched his back. "Even official warships cannot receive their orders and directions in the Snap because of the radio-density. So Administrative Alliance Headquarters is lenient with us. We do our job well; they look the other way. They cannot give us orders; neither can they supply us with weapons or provisions. Therefore we ignore certain salvage conventions and capture regulations. Stellarmen call us looters.'' He searched her for a reaction. "We are staunch defenders of the Alliance, Captain Wong, but . . .'' He raised his hand, made a fist and brought the fist against his belly. "But if we are hungry, and no Invader ship has come by—well, we take what comes past.''

"I see,'' Rydra said. "Do I understand I am taken?'' She recalled the Baron, the rapaciousness implicit in his lean figure.

Tarik's fingers opened on his stomach. "Do I look hungry?''

Rydra grinned. "You look very well fed.''

He nodded. "This has been a prosperous month. Were it not, we would not be sitting together so amiably. You are our guests for now.''

"Then you will help us repair the burned-out genera-tors?''

Tarik raised his hand again, signaling her to halt. ". . . for now,'' he repeated.

Rydra had moved forward on her seat; she sat back again.

Tarik spoke to Klik: "Bring the books.'' The jester stepped quickly away and delved into a stand beside the couches. "We live dangerously,'' Tarik went on. "Perhaps that is why we live well. We are civilized—when we have time. The name of your ship convinced me to heed the Butcher's suggestion to hook you out. Here on the *rim* we are seldom visited by a *Bard*.'' Rydra smiled as politely as she could at the pun.

Klik returned with three volumes. The covers were black with silver edging. Tarik held them up. "My favorite is the second. I was particularly struck with the long narrative *Exiles in Mist*. You tell me you have never heard of shadow-ships, yet you do know the feelings 'that loop night to bind you'—that is the line, isn't it? I confess, your third book I do not understand. But there are many references and humorous allusions to current events. We here are out of the mainstream." He shrugged. "We . . . salvaged the first from the collection of the captain of an Invader transport tramp that had wandered off course. The second—well, it came from an Alliance destroyer. I believe there's an inscription on the inside cover." He opened it and read: 'For Joey on the first flight; she says so well what I have always wanted to say so much. With so much, much love, Lenia.' " He closed the cover. "Touching. The third I only acquired a month ago. I will read it several times more before I speak of it to you again. I am astounded at the coincidence that brings us together." He placed the books in his lap. "How long has the third one been out?"

"A little under a year."

"There is a fourth?"

She shook her head.

"May I inquire what literary work you are engaged in now?"

"Now, nothing. I've done some short poems that my publisher wants to put out in a collection, but I want to wait until I have another large, sustained work to balance them."

Tarik nodded. "I see. But your reticence deprives us of great pleasure. Should you be moved to write, I will be honored. At meals we have music, some dramatic or comic entertainment, directed by clever Klik. If you would give us prologue or epilogue with what fancy you choose, you will have an appreciative audience." He extended his brown, hard hand. Appreciation is not a warm feeling, Rydra realized, but cool, and makes your back relax at the same time that you smile. She took his hand.

"Thank you, Tarik," she said.

"I thank you," Tarik returned. "Having your good will, I shall release your crew. They are free to wander Jebel as my own men are." His brown gaze shifted and she released his hand. "The Butcher." He nodded and she turned.

The convict who had been with him on the ramp now stood on the step below.

"What was that blot that lay toward Rigel?" Tarik asked.

"Alliance running, Invader tracking."

Tarik's face furrowed, then relaxed. "No, let them both pass. We eat well enough this month. Why upset our guests with violence? This is Rydra——"

The Butcher brought his right fist cracking into his left palm. People below turned. She jumped at the sound, and with her eyes she tried to strip meaning from the faintly quivering muscles, the fixed, full-lipped face: lancing but inarticulate hostility; an outrage at stillness, a fear of motion halted, safety in silence furious with movement—

Now Tarik spoke again, voice lower, slower, harsh. "You're right. But what whole man is not of two minds on any matter of moment, eh, Captain Wong?" He rose. "Butcher, pull us closer to their trajectory. Are they an hour out? Good. We will watch a while, then trounce"—he paused and smiled at Rydra—"the Invaders."

The Butcher's hands came apart, and Rydra saw relief (or release) ease his arms. He breathed again.

"Ready Jebel, and I will escort our guest to where she may watch."

Without response, the Butcher strode to the bottom of the steps. Those nearest had overheard, and the information saturated the room. Men and women rose from their benches. One upset his drinking horn. Rydra saw the girl who had served them in the infirmary run with a towel to sop the drink.

At the head of the gallery stairs she looked over the balcony rail at the commons below, empty now.

"Come." Tarik motioned her through the columns toward the darkness and the stars. "The Alliance ship is coming through there." He pointed to a bluish cloud. "We have equipment that can penetrate a good deal of this mist, but I doubt the Alliance ship even knows it is being tracked by Invaders." He moved to a desk and pressed a raised disk. Two dots of light flashed in the mist. "Red for Invaders," Tarik explained. "Blue for Alliance. Our little spider-boats will be yellow. You can follow the progress of the encounter from here. All our sensory evaluations and sensory perceptors and navigators remain on Jebel and direct the major strategy by remote control, so formations remain consistent. But within a limited range, each spider-boat battles for itself. It's fine sport for the men."

"What sort of ships are these you hunt?" She was amused that the slight archaic tone that perfused Tarik's speech had begun to affect hers.

"The Alliance ship is a military supply ship. The Invader is tracking her with a small destroyer."

"How far apart are they?"

"They should engage each other in about twenty minutes."

"And you are going to wait sixty minutes before you . . . trounce the Invaders?"

Tarik smiled. "A supply ship doesn't have much chance against a destroyer."

"I know." She could see him waiting, behind the smile, for her to object. She looked for objection in herself, but it was blocked by a clot of tiny singing sounds on an area of her tongue smaller than a coin: Babel-17. They defined a concept of exactingly necessary expedient curiosity that became in any other language a clumsy string of polysyllables. "I've never watched a stellar skirmish," she said.

"I would have you come in my flagship, but I know that the little danger there is, is danger enough. From here you can follow the whole battle much more clearly."

Excitement caught her up. "I'd like to go with you." She hoped he might change his mind.

"Stay here," Tarik said. "The Butcher rides with me this time. Here's a sensory helmet if you wish to view the stasis currents. Though with combat weapons, there's so much electromagnetic confusion I doubt that even a reduction would mean much." A run of lights flashed across the desk top. "Excuse me. I go to review my men and check my cruiser." He bowed shortly. "Your crew has revived. They will be directed up here and you may explain their status as my guests however you see fit.''

As Tarik walked to the steps, she looked back to the glittering view-screen and a few moments later thought: What an amazing graveyard they have on this hulk; it must take fifty discorporate souls to do all the sensory reading for Tarik and its spider-boats—in Basque again. She looked back and saw the translucent shapes of her Eye, Ear, and Nose across the gallery.

"Am I glad to see you!" she said. "I didn't know whether Tarik had discorporate facilities!"

"Does it!" Came the Basque response. "We'll take you on a trip through the Underworld here. Captain. They treat you like the lords of Hades."

From the speaker came Tarik's voice: "Hear this: the strategy is Asylum. Asylum. Repeat a third time, Asylum. Inmates gather to face Caesar. Psychotics ready at the K-ward gate. Neurotics gather before the R-ward gate. Criminally insane prepare for discharge at the T-ward gate. All right, drop your straitjackets."

At the bottom of the hundred-foot screen appeared three groups of yellow lights—the three groups of spider-boats that would attack the Invader once it had overtaken the Alliance supply ship. "Neurotics advance. Maintain contact to avoid separation anxiety." The middle group began to move slowly forward. On the under-speakers now, punctuated with static, Rydra heard lower voices as the men began to report back to the Navigators on Jebel:

Keep us on course, now, Kippi, and don't get shook.

Sure thing. Hawk, will you get your reports back on time?

Ease up. My caper-unit keeps sticking.

Who told you to leave without getting overhauled?

Come on, ladies, be kind to us for once.

Hey, Pigfoot, you want to be lobbed in high or low?

Low, hard, and fast. Don't hang me up.

You just get your reports in, honeybunch.

Over the main speaker Tarik said: "The Hunter and the Hunted have engaged——" The red light and the blue light started blinking on the screen. Calli, Ron, and Mollya came from the head of the steps.

"What's going . . . ?" Calli started, but silenced at a gesture from Rydra.

"That red light's an Invader ship. We're attacking it in a few moments. We're the yellow lights down here." She left the explanation at that.

"Good luck, us," Mollya said, dryly.

In five minutes there was only the red light left. By now Brass had clanked up the steps to join them. Tarik announced: "The Hunter has become the Hunted. Let the criminally-insane schiz out." The yellow group on the left started forward, spreading apart.

That Invader looks pretty big, there, Hawk.

Don't worry. She'll run us out tough.

Hell. I don't like hard work. Got my reports yet?

Right-o. Pigfoot, stop jamming Ladybird's beam!

Okay, okay, okay. Did anyone check out tractor's nine and ten?

You think of everything at the right time, don't you?

Just curious. Don't the spiral look pretty back there?

"Neurotics proceed with delusions of grandeur. Napoleon Bonaparte take the lead. Jesus Christ bring up the rear." The ships on the right moved forward now in diamond formation. "Stimulate severe depression, non-comunicative, with repressed hostility."

Behind her she heard young voices. The Slug herded the platoon up the steps. Arriving, they quieted before the vast representation of night. The explanation of the battle filtered back among the children in whispers.

"Commence the first psychotic episode." Yellow lights ran forward into the darkness.

The Invader must have spotted them at last, for it began to move away. The gross bulk could not outrun the spiders unless it jumped currents. And there was not enough leeway to check out. The three groups of yellow lights—formed, unformed, and dispersed—drew closer. After three minutes, the Invader stopped running. On the screen there was a sudden shower of red lights. It had released its own barrage of cruisers which also separated into the three standard attack groups.

"The life goal has become dispersed," Tarik announced. "Do not become despondent."

Come on, let them babies try and get us!
Remember, Kippi, low, fast, and hard!
If we scare them into offensive, we got it made!

"Prepare to penetrate hostile defense mechanisms. All right. Administer medication!"

The formation of the Invader's cruiser, however, was not offensive. A third of them fanned horizontally across the stars, the second group combed over their paths at a sixty degree angle, and the third group moved through another rotation of sixty degrees so they made a three-way defensive grid before the mother ship. The red cruisers doubled back on themselves at the end of their run and swept out again, netting the space before the Invader with small ships.

"Take heed. The enemy has tightened its defense mechanisms."

What's with this new formation, anyway?
We'll get through. You worried——?

Static chopped out one speaker.

Damn, they strafed Pigfoot!
Pull me back, Kippi. There you go. Pigfoot?
Did you see how they got him? Hey, let's go.

"Administer active therapy to the right. Be as directive as you can. Let the center enjoy the pleasure principle. And the left go hang."

Rydra watched, fascinated, as yellow lights engaged the red which still swept hypnotically along their grid, net, web—

Webbing! The picture flipped over in her mind and the other side had all the missing lines. The grid was identical to the three-way web she had torn off the hammock hours before, with the added factor of timing, because the strands were the paths of ships, not strings; but it worked the same way. She snatched up a microphone from the desk. "Tarik!" The word took forever to slide from post-dental, to palital stop, beside the sounds that danced through her brain now. She barked at the Navigators beside her: "Calli, Mollya, Ron, coordinate the battle area for me."

"Huh?" said Calli. "All right." He began to adjust the dial of the stellarimeter in his palm. Slow motion, she thought. They're all moving in slow motion. She knew what should be done, must be done, and watched the situation changing.

"Rydra Wong, Tarik is occupied," came the Butcher's gravelly voice.

Calli said over his shoulder: "Coordinates 3-B, 41-F, and 9-K. Pretty quick, huh?"

It seemed she'd asked for them an hour ago. "Butcher, did you get those coordinates down? Now look, in ... twenty-seven seconds a cruiser will pass through——" She gave a three number location. "Hit it with your closest neurotics." While she waited for a response, she saw where the next hit must lie, "Forty seconds off, starting—eight, nine, ten, *now*, an Invader cruiser will pass through——" another location. "—Get it with whatever's nearest. Is the first ship out of commission?"

"Yes, Captain Wong."

Her amazement and relief took no breath. At least the Butcher was listening; she gave the coordinates of three more ships in the 'web.' "Now hit them straight on and watch things fall apart!"

As she put the microphone down, Tarik's voice announced: "Advance for group therapy!"

The yellow spider-boats surged into the darkness again. Where there should have been Invaders, there were empty holes; where there should have been reinforcements, there was confusion. First one, then another, red cruiser fled its position.

The yellow lights were through. The flare of a vibra-blast shattered the red glow of the Invader ship.

Ratt jumped up and down, holding on to Carlos' and Flop's shoulder. "Hey, we won!" the midget Reconversion Engineer cried out. "We won!"

The platoon murmured to one another. Rydra felt oddly far away. They talked so slowly, taking such impossible time to say what could be so quickly delineated by a few simple—

"Are you all right, Ca'tain?" Brass put his yellow paw around her shoulder.

She tried to speak, but it came out a grunt. She staggered against his arm.

The Slug had turned now. "You feel well?" he asked.

"Sssssss," and realized that she didn't know how to say it in Babel-17. Her mouth bit into the shape and feel of English. "Sick," she said. "Jesus, I feel sick."

As she said it, the dizziness passed.

"Maybe you better lie down?" suggested the Slug.

She shook her head. The tenseness in her shoulders and back, the nausea was leaving. "No. I'm all right. I just got a little too excited, I think."

"Sit down a minute," Brass said, letting her lean against the desk. But she pushed herself upright.

"Really, I'm O.K. now." She took a deep breath. "See?" She pulled from under Brass' arm. "I'm going to take a walk. I'll feel better then." Still unsteady, she started away. She felt their wariness to let her go, but suddenly she wanted to be somewhere else. She continued across the gallery floor.

Her breath got back to normal when she reached the upper levels. Then, from six different directions, hallways joined with rolling ramps to descend toward other floors. She stopped, confused over which way to take, then turned at a sound.

A group of Tarik's crew was crossing the corridor. The Butcher, among them, paused to lean against the door frame. He grinned at her, seeing her confusion, and pointed to the right. She didn't feel like speaking, so merely smiled and touched her forehead in salute. As she started toward the righthand ramp, the meaning behind his grin surprised her. There was the pride of their joint success (which had allowed her to remain silent), yes; and a direct pleasure at offering her his wordless aid. But that was all. The expected amusement over someone who had lost her way was missing. Its presence would not have annoyed her. But its absence charmed. Also it fit the angular brutality she had watched before, as well as the great animal grace of him.

She was still smiling when she reached the commons.

11

~~~~~~

She leaned on the catwalk railing to watch the activity in the cradle of the loading dock curving below. "Slug, take the kids down to give a hand with those carter-winches. Tarik said they could use some help."

Slug guided the platoon to the chair-lift that dropped into Jebel's pit:

". . . all right, when you get down there, go over to that man in the red shirt and ask him to put you to work. Yeah, work. Don't look so surprised, stupid. Kile, strap yourself in, will you. It's two hundred and fifty feet down and a little hard on your head if you fall. Hey, you two, cut it out. I know he started first. Just get down there and be constructive . . ."

Rydra watched machinery, organic supplies—Alliance and Invader—handed in from the dismantling crews that worked over the ruins of the two ships, and their swarm of cruisers; the stacked, sorted crates were piled along the loading area.

"We'll be jettisonning the cruiser ships shortly. I'm afraid *Rimbaud* will have to go, too. Is there anything you'd like to salvage before we dump it, Captain?" She turned at Tarik's voice.

"There are some important papers and recordings I have to get. I'll leave my platoon here and take my officers with me."

"Very well." Tarik joined her at the railing. "As soon as we finish here, I'll send a work-crew with you in case there's anything large you want to bring back."

"That won't be . . ." she began. "Oh, I see. You need fuel, don't you."

Tarik nodded. "And stasis components, also spare parts for our own spider-boats. We will not touch the *Rimbaud* until you have finished with it."

"I see. I guess that's only fair."

"I'm impressed," Tarik went on to change the subject, "with your method of breaking the Invader's defense net. That particular formation has always given us some trouble. The Butcher tells me you tore it apart in less than five minutes, and we only lost one spider. That's a record. I didn't know you were a master strategist as well as a poet. You have many talents. It is lucky that Butcher took your call, though. I would not have had sense enough to follow your instructions just on the spur of the moment. Had the results not been so praiseworthy, I would have been put out with him. But then his decisions have never yet brought me less than profit." He looked across the pit.

On a suspended platform in the center, the ex-convict lounged, silent overseer to the operations below.

"He's a curious man," Rydra said. "What was he in prison for?"

"I have never asked," Tarik said, raising his chin. "He has never told me. There are many curious persons on Jebel. And privacy is important in so small a space. Oh, yes. In a month's time you will learn how tiny the Mountain is."

"I forgot myself," Rydra apologized. "I shouldn't have inquired."

An entire foresection of a blasted Invader's cruiser was being dragged through the funnel on a twenty-foot wide, pronged conveyor. Dismantlers swarmed up the side with bolt punches and laser spots. Gig-cranes caught on the smooth hull and began to turn it slowly.

A workman at the port-disk suddenly cried out and swung hastily aside. His tools clattered down the bulkhead. The port-disk swung up and a figure in a silver skin suit dropped the twenty-five feet to the conveyor belt, rolled between two prongs, regained footing, leaped down the next ten-foot drop to the floor, and ran. The hood slipped from her head to release shoulder-length brown hair which swung wildly as she changed her course to avoid a trundling sludge. She moved fast, yet with a certain awkwardness. Then Rydra recognized that what she had taken for paunchiness in the fleeing Invader was at least a seven months' pregnancy. A mechanic flung a wrench at her, but she dodged so that it deflected off her hip. She was running toward an open space between the stacked supplies.

Then the air was cut by a vibrant hiss: the Invader stopped, sat down hard on the floor as the hiss repeated; she pitched to the side, kicked out one leg, kicked again.

On the tower, the Butcher put his vibra-gun back in the holster.

"That was unnecessary," Tarik said, with shocking softness.

"Couldn't we have . . ." and there seemed to be nothing to suggest. On Tarik's face was pain and curiosity. The pain, she realized, was not at the double death on the deck below, but the chagrin of a gentleman caught at something ugly. His curiosity was at her reaction. And it might be worth her life to react to the twisting in her stomach. She watched him preparing to speak: he was going to say—and so she said it for him—: "They will use pregnant women as pilots on fighting ships. Their reflexes are faster." She watched for him to relax, saw the relaxation begin.

The Butcher was already stepping from the chair-lift onto the catwalk. He came toward them, banging his fist against his corded thigh with impatience. "They should ray everything before they take it on. They won't listen. Second time in two months now." He grunted.

Below, Jebel's men and her platoon mingled over the body.

"They will next time." Tarik's voice was still soft and cool. "Butcher, you seemed to have pricked Captain Wong's interest. She was wondering what sort of a fellow you were, and I really couldn't tell her. Perhaps you can explain why you had to——"

"Tarik," Rydra said. Her eyes, seeking him, snagged on the Butcher's dark gaze. "I'd like to go to my ship now and see to it before you start salvaging."

Tarik exhaled the rest of the breath he'd held since the hiss of the vibra-gun. "Of course."

"No, not a monster, Brass." She unlocked the door to the captain's cabin of the *Rimbaud* and stepped through. "Just expedient. It's just like . . ." And she said a lot more to him till his fang-distended mouth sneered and he shook his head.

"Talk to me in English, Ca'tain. I don't understand you."

She took the dictionary from the console and placed it on top of the charts. "I'm sorry," she said. "This stuff is wicked. Once you learn it, it makes everything so easy. Get those tapes out of the playback. I want to run through them again."

"What are they?" Brass brought them over.

"Transcriptions of the last Babel-17 dialogues at the War Yards just before we took off." She put them on the spindle and started the first playing.

A melodious torrent rippled through the room, caught her up in ten and twenty second bursts she could understand. The plot to undermine TW-55 was delineated with hallucinatory vividness. When she reached a section she could not understand, she was left shaking against the wall of non-communication. While she listened, while she understood, she moved through psychedelic perceptions. When understanding left, her breath left her lungs with shock, and she had to blink, shake her head, once accidentally bit her tongue, before she was free again to comprehend.

"Captain Wong?"

It was Ron. She turned her head, aching slightly now, to face him.

"Captain Wong, I don't want to disturb you."

"That's all right," she said. "What is it?"

"I found this in the Pilot's Den." He held up a small spool of tape.

Brass was still standing by the door. "What was it doing in my part of the shi'?"

Ron's features fought with each other for an expression. "I just played it back with Slug. It's Captain Wong's—or

somebody's—request to Flight Clearance back at the War
Yards for take off, and the all clear signal to Slug to get ready
to blast.''

"I see," Rydra said. She took the spool. Then she
frowned. "This reel is from my cabin. I use the three-lobed
spools I brought with me from the University. All the other
machines on the ship are supplied with four-lobed ones. That
tape came from this machine here.''

"So," Brass said, "a''arently somebody snuck in and
made it when you were out.''

"When I'm out, this place is locked so tight a discorporate
flea couldn't crawl under the door." She shook her head. "I
don't like this. I don't know where I'll be fouled up next.
Well''—she stood up—"at least I know what I have to do
about Babel-17 now.''

"What's that?" Brass asked. Slug had come to the door
and was looking over Ron's flowered shoulder.

Rydra looked over the crew. Discomfort or distrust,
which was worst? "I really can't tell you now, can I?" she
said. "It's that simple." She walked to the door. "I wish I
could. But it would be a little silly after this whole business.''

"But I would rather speak to Tarik!"

Klik ruffled his feathers and shrugged. "Lady, I would
honor your desire above all others' on the mountain, save
Tarik's. And it is Tarik's desire that you now counter. He
wishes not to be disturbed. He is plotting Jebel's destina-
tion over the next time-cycle. He must judge the currents
carefully, and weigh even the weights of the stars about us. It
is an arduous task, and——''

"Then where's the Butcher? I'll ask him, but I would
prefer to talk directly with——''

The jester pointed with a green talon. "He is in the
biology theatre. Go down through the commons and take the
first lift to level twelve. It is directly to your left.''

"Thank you." She headed toward the gallery steps.

At the top of the lift she found the huge iris door, and
pressed the entrance disk. Leaves folded, and she blinked in
green light.

His round head and mildly humped shoulders were silhouetted before a bubbling tank in which a tiny figure floated: the spray of bubbles that rose about the form deflated on the feet, caught in the crossed curved hands like sparks, frothed the bent head, and foamed in the brush of birth-hair that swirled up in the miniature currents.

The Butcher turned, saw her, and said, "It died." He nodded with vigorous belligerence. "It was alive until five minutes ago. Seven and a half months. It should have lived. It was strong enough!" His left fist cracked against his right palm, as she had seen him do in the commons. Shaking muscles stilled. He thumbed toward an operating table where the Invader's body lay—sectioned. "Badly hurt before she got out. Internal organs messed up. A lot of abdominal necrosis all the way through." He turned his hand so the thumb now pointed over his shoulder to the drifting homunculus, and the gesture that had seemed rough took on an economical grace. "Still—it should have lived."

He switched off the light in the tank and the bubbles ceased. He stepped from behind the laboratory table. "What the Lady want?"

"Tarik is planning Jebel's route for the next months. Could you ask him . . ." She stopped. Then she asked, "Why."

Ron's muscles, she thought, were living cords that snapped and sang out their messages. On this man, muscles were shields to hold the world out, the man in. And something inside was leaping up again and again, striking the shield from behind. The scored belly shifted, the chest contracted over a let breath; the brow smoothed, then creased again.

"Why?" she repeated. "Why did you try to save the child?"

He twisted his face for answer, and his left hand circled the convict's mark on his other bicep as though it had started to sting. Then he gave up with disgust. "Died. No good any more. What the Lady want?"

What leaped and leaped retreated now, and so did she. "I want to know if Tarik will take me to Administrative Alliance Headquarters. I have to deliver some important information concerning the Invasion. My pilot tells me the Specelli Snap runs within ten hyperstatic units, which a spider-boat could make, so Jebel could remain in radio-dense space all the way. If Tarik will escort me to Headquarters, I will guarantee his protection and a safe return to the denser part of the Snap."

He eyed her. "All the way down the Dragon's Tongue?"

"Yes. That's what Brass told me the tip of the Snap was called."

"Protection guaranteed?"

"That's right. I'll show you my credentials from General Forester of the Alliance if you . . ."

But he waved for her silence. "Tarik." He spoke into the wall intercom.

The speaker was directional so she couldn't hear the answer.

"Make Jebel go down the Dragon's Tongue during the first cycle."

There was either questioning or objection.

"Go down the Tongue and it'll be good."

He nodded to the unintelligible whisper, then said, "It died," and switched off. "All right. Tarik will take Jebel to Headquarters."

Amazement undercut her initial disbelief. It was an amazement she would have felt before when he responded so unquestioningly to her plan to destroy the Invader's defense, had not Babel-17 precluded such feelings. "Well, thanks," she began, "but you haven't even asked me . . ." Then she decided to phrase the whole thing another way.

But the Butcher made a fist:

"Knowing what ships to destroy, and ships are destroyed." He banged his fist against his chest. "Now to go down the Dragon's Tongue, Jebel go down the Dragon's Tongue." He banged his chest again.

She wanted to question, but looked at the dead fetus turning in dark liquid behind him and said instead, "Thank you, Butcher." As she stepped through the iris door, she mulled over what he had said to her, trying to frame some explanation of his actions. Even the rough way in which his words fell—

His *words!*
It struck her at once, and she hurried down the corridor.

III

~~~~~~

"Brass, he can't say 'I'!" She leaned across the table, surprised curiosity impelling her excitement.

The pilot locked his claws around his drinking horn. The wooden tables across the commons were being set up for the evening meal.

"Me, my, mine, myself. I don't think he can say any of those either. Or think them. I wonder where the hell he's from."

"You know any language where there's no word for 'I'?"

"I can think of a couple where it isn't used often, but no one that doesn't even have the concept, if only hanging around in a verb ending."

"Which all means what?"

"A strange man with a strange way of thinking. I don't know why, but he's aligned himself with me, sort of my ally on this trip and a go-between with Tarik. I'd like to understand, so I won't hurt him."

She looked around the commons at the bustle of preparation. The girl who had brought them chicken was glancing at her now, wondering, still afraid, fear melting to curiosity which brought her two tables nearer, then curiosity evaporating to indifference, and she was off for more spoons from the wall drawer.

She wondered what would happen if she translated her perceptions of people's movement and muscle tics into Babel-17. It was not only a language, she understood now, but a flexible matrix of analytical possibilities where the same 'word' defined the stresses in a webbing of medical bandage, or a defensive grid of spaceships. What would it do with the tensions and yearnings in a human face? Perhaps the flicker of eyelids and fingers would become mathematics, without meaning. Or perhaps— While she thought, her mind changed gears into the headlong compactness of Babel-17. And she swept her eyes around the—voices.

Expanding and defining through one another, not the voices themselves, but the minds making the voices, braiding with one another, so that the man entering the hall now she knew to be the grieving brother

She sat in the great commons while men and women filed in for the evening meal, and was aware of so much more. of Pigfoot, and the girl who'd served them was in love, so in love with the dead youth from the discorporate sector who tickled her dreams turning

about the general hunger, a belly beast with teeth in one man, a lazy pool in another, now the familiar rush of adolescent confusion as the *Rimbaud*'s platoon came pummeling in, driven by the deep concern of Slug, and further over amidst ebullience, hunger, and love, a *fear!* It gonged in the hall, flashed red in the indigo tide, and she searched for Tarik or the Butcher because their names were in the fear, but found neither in the room; instead, a thin man named Geoffry Cord in whose brain crossed wires sparked and sputtered *Make death with the knife I have*

sheathed to my leg, and again *With my steel tongue make me a place in an eyrie high on Jebel,* and the minds about him, groping and hungering, *They set her place, brought first a flagon, then bread, which she saw and smiled at but was seeing so much else.*

mumbling over humor and hurt, loving a little and groping for more, all crosshatched with relaxation one way at the coming meal, and in others anticipation at what clever Klik would present that evening, the minds of the actors of the pantomime keyed to performance while they perused the spectators whom, at an earlier hour, they had worked and slept with, one elderly navigator with a geometrical head hurrying to give the girl, who was to play in the play at being in love, a silver clasp he had melted and scribed himself to see if she would play at loving him, yet through all this her mind circled back to the alarm of Geoffry Cord, *I must act this evening as the actors close*, and unable to focus on anything but his urgency, she watched him roil and ravel through his plotting, to hurry forward when the pantomime began as if he wanted to get a closer look as many would do, slip beside the table where Tarik would be sitting, then blade between Tarik's ribs with his serpent fang, grooved metal ran with paralytic poison, then chomp down on his hollow tooth that was filled with hypnotic drugs so that when he was taken prisoner they would think he

Around her people were sitting, relaxing, while the serving people hurried to the food counter where the roasts and fried fruit steamed.

was under somebody else's control, and at last he would release a wild story, implanted below the level of the hypnotics by many painful hours under the personafix, that he was under the Butcher's control; then somehow he would contrive to be alone with the Butcher and bite the Butcher's hand or wrist or leg, injecting the same hypnotic drugs that poisoned his own mouth and rend the hulking convict helpless, and he would control him, and when the Butcher ultimately became Jebel's ruler after the assassination, Geoffry Cord would become the Butcher's lieutenant as the Butcher was now Tarik's, and when Tarik's Jebel was the Butcher's Jebel, Geoffry would control the Butcher the same way he suspected the Butcher controlled Tarik, and there would be a reign of harshness and all strangers expelled from the berg to death by vacuum, and they would fall mightily on all ships, Invader, Alliance, or Shadow in the Snap, and Rydra tore her mind from his and swept the brief surface of

She saw so much more than the little demonic jester on the stage saying, "Before our evening's entertainment I wish to ask our guest, Captain Wong, if she would speak some few words or perhaps recite for us." And she knew with a very small part of her mind —but it took no more—that she must use this chance to denounce him.

Tarik and the Butcher, and saw no hypnotics, but also that they suspected no treachery and her own delayed fear, taking her from what she felt in her slipping and lapping with doubled and halved voice and no yes, she was able, even as she walked to pick the words and images that would drive and push him to her betrayal and no yes, once struck by his fear and rebounding, she brought herself back to a single line that scribed through both perception and action, speech and communication, both one now, picking down sounds that would persuade with the deliberation this lengthened time lent and she reached the platform beside the gorgeous beast, Klik, and mounted, hearing the voices that sang in the hall's silence, and tossed her words now from the sling of her vibrant voice, so that they hung outside her, and she watched them and watched his watching: the rhythm which was barely intricate to most ears in the commons was to him painful because it was timed to the processes of his body, to jar and strike against them . . . and she was surprised he had held up this long.

The realisation momentarily blotted everything else, but then returned to its proper size, for she knew she could not let Cord stop her from getting to Headquarters, so she stood up and walked to the stage at the end of the commons, picking from Cord's mind as she walked a deadly blade so quickly to fit into the cracks of Geoffrey Cord.

Her fear broke from her vast ship-picture while she felt schismic rages of him and still would survive it and found his fear as porous, porous as a sponge.

"All right, Cord,
to be lord of this black barrick,
Tarik's, you need more than jackal lore,
or a belly full of murder and jelly knees.
Open your mouth and your hands. To understand
power, use your wit, please.
Ambition like a liquid ruby stains
your brain, birthed in the cervixed will

to kill, swung in the arc of death's again,
you name yourself victim each time you fill
with swill the skull's cup lipping murder. It
predicts your fingers' movement toward the blade
long laid against the leather sheath cord-fixed
to pick the plan your paling fingers made;
you stayed in safety, missing worlds of wonder,
under the lithe hiss of the personafix
inflicting false memories to make them blunder
while thunder cracks the change of Tarik.
You stick pins in peaches, place your strange
blade, ranged with a grooved tooth, while the long
and strong lines of my meaning make your mind change
from fulgent to frangent. Now you hear the wrong
cord-song, to instruct you. Assassin,
pass in . . ."

She looked directly at Geoffry Cord. Geoffry Cord looked directly at her and shrieked.

The scream snapped something. She had been thinking in Babel-17 and choosing her English words with it. But now she was thinking in English again.

Geoffry Cord jerked his head sideways, black hair shaking, flung his table over, and ran, raging, toward her. The drugged knife which she had seen only through his mind was out and aimed at her stomach.

She jumped back, kicked at his wrist as he vaulted the platform edge, missed, but struck his face. He fell backwards, rolling on the floor.

Gold, silver, amber: Brass was running from his side of the room. Silver-haired Tarik was coming from the other, his cloak billowing. And the Butcher had already reached her, was between her and the uncoiling Cord.

"What is this?" Tarik demanded.

Cord was on one knee, knife still poised. His black eyes went from vibra-gun muzzle to vibra-gun muzzle, then to Brass' unsheathed claws. He froze.

"I don't appreciate attacks on my guests."

"That knife is meant for you, Tarik," she panted.

"Check the records of Jebel's personafix. He was going to kill you and get the Butcher under hypnotic control, and take over Jebel."

"Oh," Tarik said. "One of those." He turned to the Butcher. "It was time for another one, wasn't it? About once every six months. I'm again grateful to you, Captain Wong."

The Butcher stepped forward and took the knife from Cord, whose body seemed frozen, whose eyes danced. Rydra listened to Cord's breath measure out the silence, while the Butcher, holding the knife by the blade, examined it. The blade itself, in the Butcher's heavy fingers, was printed steel. The handle, a seven inch length of bone, was rigid, runneled, and stained with walnut dye.

With his free hand, the Butcher caught his fingers in Cord's black hair. Then, not particularly quickly, he pushed the knife to the hilt into Cord's right eye, handle first.

The scream became a gurgle. The flailing hands fell from the Butcher's shoulders. Those sitting close stood.

Rydra's heart banged twice to break her ribs. "But you didn't even check. . . . Suppose I was wrong . . . Maybe there was more to it than . . ." Her tongue wagged through the meaningless protests. And maybe her heart had stopped.

The Butcher, both hands bloody, looked at her coldly. "He moved with a knife on Jebel toward Tarik or Lady and he dies." Right fist ground on left palm, now soundless with red lubricant.

"Miss Wong," Tarik said, "from what I've seen, there's little doubt in my mind that Cord was certainly dangerous. I'm sure there's not much in yours, either. You are highly useful. I am highly obliged. I hope this trip down the Dragon's Tongue proves propitious. The Butcher had just told me it was at your request that we are going."

"Thank you, but . . ." Her heart was pounding again. She tried to form some clause to hang from the hook of 'but' still hesitant in her mouth. Instead she got very sick, pitched forward, half blinded. The Butcher caught her on red palms.

The round, warm, blue room again. But alone, and she

was at last able to think about what had happened in the commons. It was not what she'd repeatedly tried to describe to Mocky. It was what Mocky had repeatedly insisted to her: telepathy. But, apparently, telepathy was the nexus of old talent and a new way of thinking. It opened worlds of perception, of action. Then why was she sick? She recalled how time slowed when her mind worked under Babel-17, how her mental processes speeded up. If there was a corresponding increase in her physiological functions, her body might not be up to the strain.

The tapes from the *Rimbaud* had told her the next 'sabotage' attempt would be at Administrative Alliance Headquarters. She wanted to get there with the language, the vocabulary and grammar, give it to them, and retire. She was almost ready to hand over the search for this mysterious speaker. But no, not quite, there was still something, something to be heard and spoken. . . .

Sick and falling, she snagged on bloody finger, woke starting. The Butcher's egoless brutality, hammered linear by what she could not know, less than primitive, was for all its horror, still human. Though bloody handed, he was safer than the precision of the world linguistically corrected. What could you say to a man who could not say 'I'? What could he say to her? Tarik's cruelties, kindnesses, existed at the articulate limits of civilization. But this red bestiality fascinated her!

IV

She rose from the hammock, this time unsnapping the bandage. She'd felt better nearly an hour, but she had lain still thinking most of the time. The ramp tilted to her feet.

When the infirmary wall solidified behind her, she paused in the corridor. The airflow pulsed like breath. Her translucent slacks brushed the tops of her bare feet. The neckline of her black silk blouse lay loose on her shoulders.

She had rested well into Jebel's night shift. During a period of high activity, the sleeping time was staggered, but when they merely moved from location to location, there were hours when nearly the whole population slept.

Rather than head toward the commons, she turned down an unfamiliar sloping tunnel. White light diffused from the floor, became amber fifty feet on, then amber became orange— she stopped and looked at her hands in orange light—and forty feet further, the orange light was red. Then . . .

Blue.

The space opened around her, the walls slanting back, the ceiling rising into darkness too high for her to see. The air flickered and blotted with the after-image from the change in color. Insubstantial mists plus her unsettled eyes made her turn to orient herself.

A man was silhouetted against the red entrance to the hall. "Butcher?"

He walked toward her, blue light fogging his features as he neared. He stopped, nodded.

"I decided to take a walk when I felt better," she explained. "What part of the ship is that?"

"Discorporate quarters."

"I should have known." They fell in step with one another. "Are you just wandering around, too?"

He shook his heavy head. "An alien ship passes close to Jebel and Tarik wants its sensory vectors."

"Alliance or Invader?"

The Butcher shrugged. "Only to know that it is not a human ship."

There were nine species among the five explored galaxies with interstellar travel. Three had allied themselves definitely with the Alliance. Four had sided with the Invaders. Two were not committed.

They had gone so far into the discorporate sector, nothing seemed solid. The walls were blue mist without corners. The echoing crackle of transference energies caused distant lightning, and her eyes were deviled by half-remembered ghosts, who had always passed moments ago, yet were never there.

"How far do we go?" she asked, having decided to walk with him, thinking as she spoke: If he doesn't know the word for 'I', how can he understand 'we'?

Understanding or not, he answered, "Soon." Then he looked directly at her with dark, heavy ridged eyes and asked, "Why?"

The tone of his voice was so different, she knew he was not referring to anything in their exchange during the past few minutes. She cast in her mind for anything she had done that might strike him as perplexing.

He repeated, "Why?"

"Why what, Butcher?"

"Why the saving of Tarik from Cord?"

There was no objection in his question, only ethical curiosity. "Because I like him and because I need him to get me to Headquarters and I would feel sort of funny if I'd let him . . ." She stopped. "Do you know who 'I' am?"

He shook his head.

"Where do you come from, Butcher? What planet were you born on?"

He shrugged. "The head," he said, after a moment, "they said there was something wrong with the brain."

"Who?"

"The doctors."

Blue fog drifted between them.

"The doctors on Titin?" she hazarded.

The Butcher nodded.

"Then why didn't they put you in a hospital instead of a prison?"

"The brain is not crazy, they said. This hand"—he held up his left—"kill four people in three days. This hand"—he raised the other—"kill seven. Blow up four buildings with thermite. The foot"—he slapped his left leg—"kicked in the head of the guard at the Telechron Bank. There's a lot of money there, too much to carry. Carry maybe four hundred thousand credits. Not much."

"You robbed the Telechron Bank of four hundred thousand credits!"

"Three days, eleven people, four buildings: all for four

hundred thousand credits. But Titin"—his face twisted—
"was not fun at all."

"So I'd heard. How long did it take for them to catch you?"

"Six months."

Rydra whistled. "I take my hat off to you, if you could keep out of their hands that long, after a bank robbery. And you know enough biotics to perform a difficult Caesarean section and keep the fetus alive. There's something in that head."

"The doctors say the brain not stupid."

"Look, you and I are going to talk to each other. But first I have to teach"—she stopped—"the brain something."

"What?"

"About *you* and *I*. You must hear the words a hundred times a day. Don't you ever wonder what they mean?"

"Why? Most things make sense without them."

"Hey, speak in whatever language you grew up with."

"No."

"Why not? I want to see if it's one I know anything about."

"The doctors say there's something wrong with the brain."

"All right. What did they say was wrong?"

"Aphasia, alexia, amnesia."

"Then you were pretty messed up." She frowned. "Was that before or after the bank robbery?"

"Before."

She tried to order what she had learned. "Something happened to you that left you with no memory, unable to speak or read, and so the first thing you did was rob the Telechron bank—which Telechron Bank?"

"On Rhea-IV."

"Oh, a small one. But, still—and you stayed free for six months. Any idea what happened to you before you lost your memory?"

The Butcher shrugged.

"I suppose they went through all the possibilities that you were working for somebody else under hypnotics. You don't know what language you spoke before you lost your memory? Well, your speech patterns now must be based on your old language or you would have learned about *I* and *you* just from picking up new words."

"Why must these sounds mean something?"

"Because you asked a question just now that I can't answer if you don't understand them."

"No." Discomfort shadowed his voice. "No. There is an answer. The words of the answer must be simpler, that's all."

"Butcher, there are certain ideas which have words for them. If you don't know the words, you can't know the ideas. And if you don't have the idea, you don't have the answer."

"The word *you* four times, yes? Still nothing unclear, and *you* means nothing."

She sighed. "That's because I was using the word phatically—ritually, without regard for its real meaning . . . as a figure of speech. Look, I asked you a question that you couldn't answer."

The Butcher frowned.

"See, you have to know what they mean to make sense out of what I just said. The best way to learn a language is by listening to it. So listen. When you"—she pointed to him—"said to me," and she pointed to herself, *"Knowing what ships to destroy, and ships are destroyed. Now to go down the Dragon's Tongue, Jebel go down the Dragon's Tongue,* twice the fist"—she touched his left hand—"banged the chest." She raised his hand to his chest. The skin was cool and smooth under her palm. "The fist was trying to tell something. And if you had used the word 'I', you wouldn't have had to use your fist. What you wanted to say was: 'You knew what ships to destroy and I destroyed the ships. You want to go down the Dragon's Tongue, I will get Jebel down the Dragon's Tongue.' "

The Butcher frowned. "Yes, the fist to tell something."

"Don't you see, sometimes you want to say things, and you're missing an idea to make them with, and missing a word to make the idea with. In the beginning was the word. That's how somebody tried to explain it once. Until something is named, it doesn't exist. And it's something the brain needs to have exist, otherwise you wouldn't have to beat your chest, or strike your fist on your palm. The brain wants it to exist; let me teach it the word."

The frown cut deeper into his face.

Just then mist blew away before them. In star-flecked blackness something drifted, flimsy and flickering. They had reached a sensory port, but it was transmitting over frequencies close to regular light. "There," said the Butcher, "there is the alien ship."

"It's from Çiribia-IV," Rydra said. "They're friendly to the Alliance."

The Butcher was surprised she'd recognized it. "A very odd ship."

"It does look funny to us, doesn't it."

"Tarik did not know where it came from." He shook his head.

"I haven't seen one since I was a kid. We had to entertain delegates from Çiribia to the Court of Outer Worlds. My mother was a translator there." She leaned on the railing and gazed at the ship. "You wouldn't think something that's so flimsy and shakes around like that would fly or make stasis jumps. But it does."

"Do they have this word, *I?*"

"As a matter of fact they have three forms of it: I-below-a-temperature-of-six-degrees-centigrade, I-between-six-and-ninety-three-degrees-centigrade, and I-above-ninety-three."

The Butcher looked confused.

"It has to do with their reproductive process," Rydra explained. "When the temperature is below six degrees they're sterile. They can only conceive when the temperature is between six and ninety-three, but to actually give birth, they have to be above ninety-three."

The Çiribian ship moved like floppy feathers across the screen.

"Maybe I can explain something to you this way; with all nine species of galaxy-hopping life forms, each as widespread as our own, each as technically intelligent, with as complicated an economy, seven of them engaged in the same war we are, still we hardly ever run into them; and they run into us or each other about as frequently: so infrequently, that

even when an experienced spaceman like Tarik passes along-
side one of their ships, he can't identify it. Wonder why?''
    ''Why?''
    ''Because compatibility factors for communication are
incredibly low. Take the Çiribians, who have enough knowledge to sail their triple-yoked poached eggs from star to star:
they have no word for 'house', 'home', or 'dwelling.' 'We
must protect our families and our homes.' When we were
preparing the treaty between the Çiribians and ourselves at
the Court of Outer Worlds, I remember that sentence took
forty-five minutes to say in Çiribian. Their whole culture is
based on heat and changes in temperature. We're just lucky
that they do know what a 'family' is, because they're the only
ones besides humans who have them. But for 'house' you
have to end up describing '. . . an enclosure that creates a
temperature discrepancy with the outside environment of so
many degrees, capable of keeping comfortable a creature with
a uniform body temperature of ninety-eight-point-six, the
same enclosure being able to lower the temperature during the
months of the warm season and raise it during the cold
season, providing a location where organic sustenance can be
refrigerated in order to be preserved, or warmed well above
the boiling point of water to pamper the taste mechanism of
the indigenous habitants who, through customs that go back
through millions of hot and cold seasons, have habitually
sought out this temperature changing device . . .' and so forth
and so on. At the end you have given them some idea of what
a 'home' is and why it is worth protecting. Give them a
schematic of the air-conditioning and central heating system,
and things begin to get through. Now: there is a huge
solar-energy conversion plant that supplies all the electrical
energy for the Court. The heat amplifying and reducing
components take up an area a little bigger than Jebel. One
Çiribian can slither through that plant and then go describe it
to another Çiribian who never saw it before so that the
second can build an exact duplicate, even to the color the
walls are painted—and this actually happened, because they
thought we'd done something ingenious with one of the
circuits and wanted to try it themselves—where each piece is

located, how big it is, in short completely describe the whole business, in nine words. Nine very small words, too.''

The Butcher shook his head. "No. A solar-heat conversion system is too complicated. These hands dismantle one, not too long ago. Too big. Not——''

"Yep, Butcher, nine words. In English it would take a couple of books full of schematics and electrical and architectural specifications. They have the proper nine words. We don't.''

"Impossible.''

"So's that.'' She pointed toward the Çiribian ship. "But it's there and flying.'' She watched the brain, both intelligent and injured, thinking. "If you have the right words,'' she said, "it saves a lot of time and makes things easier.''

After a while he asked, "What is *I?*''

She grinned. "First of all it's very important. A good deal more important than anything else. The brain will let any number of things go to pot as long as 'I' stay alive. That's because the brain is part of I. A book is, a ship is, Tarik is, the universe is, but, as you must have noticed, I am.''

The Butcher nodded. "Yes. But I am what?''

Fog closed over the view-port, misting stars and the Çiribian ship. "That's a question only you can answer.''

"You must be important too,'' the Butcher mused, "because the brain has overheard that you are.''

"Good boy!''

Suddenly he put his hand on her cheek. The cock's spur rested lightly on her lower lip. "You and I,'' the Butcher said. He moved his face close to hers. "Nobody else is here. Just you and I. But which is which?''

She nodded, cheek moving on his fingers. "You're getting the idea.'' His chest had been cool; his hand was warm. She put her hand on top of his. "Sometimes you frighten me.''

"I and me,'' the Butcher said. "Only a morphological distinction, yes? The brain figure that out before. Why does you frighten me sometimes?''

"*Do* frighten. A morphological correction. You frighten

me because you rob banks and put knife handles in people's heads, Butcher!"

"You do?" Then his surprise left. "Yes, you do, don't you. You forgot."

"But I didn't," Rydra said.

"Why does that frighten I? . . . correction, me. Overhear that too."

"Because it's something I've never done, never wanted to do, never could do. And I like you, I like your hand on my cheek, so that if you suddenly decided to put a knife handle in *my* eye, well . . ."

"Oh. You never would put a knife handle in my eye," the Butcher said. "I don't have to worry."

"You could change your mind."

"You won't." He looked at her closely. "I don't really think you're going to kill me. You know that. I know that. It's something else. Why don't I tell you something else that frightened me? Maybe you can see some pattern and you will understand then. The brain is not stupid."

His hand slid to her neck, and there was concern in his puzzled eyes. She had seen it before the moment he'd turned from the dead fetus in the biology theater. "Once . . ." she began slowly, ". . . well, there was a bird."

"Birds frighten me?"

"No. But this bird did. I was just a kid. You don't remember being a kid, do you? In most people what you were as a kid has a lot to do with what you are now."

"And what I am too?"

"Yes, me too. My doctor had gotten this bird for me as a present. It was a myna bird, which can talk. But it doesn't know what it's saying. It just repeats like a tape recorder. Only I didn't know that. A lot of times I know what people are trying to say to me, Butcher. I never understood it before, but since I've been on Jebel, I've realized it's got something to do with telepathy. Anyway, this myna bird had been trained to talk by feeding it earthworms when it said the right thing. Do you know how big an earthworm is?"

"Like so?"

"That's right. And some of them even run a few inches longer. And a myna bird is about eight or nine inches long. In other words a earthworm can be about five-sixths as long as a myna bird, which is what's important. The bird had been trained to say: Hello, Rydra, it's a fine day out and I'm happy. But the only thing this meant in the bird's mind was a rough combination of visual and olfactory sensations that translated loosely, *There's another earthworm coming.* So when I walked into the greenhouse and said hello to this myna bird, and it replied, 'Hello, Rydra, it's a fine day and I'm happy,' I knew immediately it was lying. There was another earthworm coming, that I could see and smell, and it was this thick and five-sixths as long as I was tall. And I was supposed to eat it. I got a little hysterical. I never told my doctor, because I never could figure exactly what happened until now. But when I remember, I still get shaky."

The Butcher nodded. "When you left Rhea with the money, you eventually holed up in a cave in the ice-hell of Dis. You were attacked by worms, twelve foot ones. They burrowed up out of the rocks with acid slime on their skins. You were scared, but you killed them. You rigged up an electric net from your hop-sled power source. You killed them, and when you knew you could beat them, you weren't afraid any more. The only reason you didn't eat them was because the acid made their flesh toxic. But you hadn't eaten anything for three days."

"I did? I mean . . . you did?"

"You are not frightened of the things I am frightened of. I am not frightened of the things you are frightened of. That's good, isn't it?"

"I guess so."

Gently he leaned his face against hers, then pulled away, and searched her face for a response.

"What is it that you're frightened of?" she asked.

He shook his head, not in negation but in confusion, as she saw him trying to articulate. "The baby, the baby that died," he said. "The brain afraid, afraid for you, that you would be alone."

"How afraid that you would be alone, Butcher?"

He shook his head again.

"Loneliness is not good."

She nodded.

"The brain knows that. For a long time it didn't know, but after a while it learned. Lonely on Rhea, you were, even with all the money. Lonelier on Dis; and in Titin, even with the other prisoners, you were loneliest of all. No one really understood you when you spoke to them. You did not really understand them. Maybe because they said *I* and *you* so much, and you just now are beginning to learn how important you are and I am."

"You wanted to raise the baby yourself so he would grow up and . . . speak the same language you speak? Or at any rate speak English the same way you speak it?"

"Then both not be alone."

"I see."

"It died," Butcher said. He grunted once again. "But now you are not quite so alone. I teach you to understand the others, a little. You're not stupid, and you learn fast." Now he turned fully toward her, rested his fists on her shoulder and spoke gravely. "You like me. Even when I first came on Jebel, there was something about me that you liked. I saw you do things I thought were bad, but you liked me. I told you how to destroy the Invaders defensive net, and you destroyed it, for me. I told you I wanted to go to the tip of the Dragon's Tongue, and you saw that I get there. You will do anything I ask. It's important that I know that."

"Thank you, Butcher," she said wonderingly.

"If you ever rob another bank, you will give me all the money."

Rydra laughed. "Why, thank you. Nobody ever wanted to do that for me. But I hope you don't have to rob——"

"You will kill anyone that tries to hurt me, kill them a lot worse than you ever killed anyone before."

"But you don't have to——"

'You will kill all of Jebel if it tries to take you and me apart and keep us alone."

"Oh, Butcher——" She turned from him and put her fist against her mouth. "One hell of a teacher I am! You don't understand a thing—I—*I* am talking about."

The voice, astonished and slow: "I don't understand you, you think."

She turned back to him. "But I do, Butcher! I do

understand you. Please believe that. But trust me that you have a little more to learn."

"You trust me," he said firmly.

"Then listen. Right now we've met each other halfway. I haven't really taught you about *I* and *you*. We've made up our own language, and that's what we're talking now."

"But—"

"Look, every time you've said *you* in the last ten minutes, you should have said *I*. Every time you've said *I*, you meant *you*."

He dropped his eyes to the floor, then raised them again, still without answer.

"What I talk about as *I*, you must speak of as *you*. And the other way around, don't you see?"

"Are they the same word for the same thing, that they are interchangeable?"

"No, just . . . yes! They both mean the same sort of thing. In a way they're the same."

"Then you and I are the same."

Risking confusion, she nodded.

"I suspect it. But you"—he pointed to her—"have taught me." He touched himself.

"And that's why you can't go around killing people. At least you better do a hell of a lot of thinking before you do. When you talk to Tarik, I and you still exist. With anyone you look at on the ship, or even through a view-screen, I and you are still there."

"The brain must think about that."

"You must think about that, with more than your brain."

"If I must then I will. But we are one, more than others." He touched her face again. "Because you taught me. Because with me you do not have to be afraid of anything. I have just learned, and I may make mistakes with other people; for an *I* to kill a *you* without a lot of thought is a mistake, isn't it? Do I use the words correctly now?"

She nodded.

"I will make no mistakes with you. That would be too terrible. I will make as few mistakes as I possibly can. And someday I will learn completely." Then he smiled. "Let's hope nobody tries to make any mistakes with me, though. I am sorry for them if they do, because I will probably make a mistake with them very quickly and with very little thought.''

"That's fair enough for now, I guess," Rydra said. She took his arms in her hands. "I'm glad you and I are together, Butcher." Then his arms came up and caught her against his body, and she pressed her face on his shoulder.

"I thank you," he whispered. "I thank you and thank you."

"You're warm," she said into his shoulder. "Don't let go for a little while."

When he did, she blinked up at his face through blue mist and turned all cold. "What *is* it, Butcher!"

He took her face between his hands and bent his head till amber hair brushed her forehead.

"Butcher, remember I told you I can tell what people are thinking? Well, I can tell something's wrong now, and you said I didn't have to be afraid of you, but you're scaring me now."

She raised his face. There were tears on it.

"Look, just the way something wrong with me would scare you, one thing that's going to scare hell out of me for a long time is something wrong with you. Tell me what it is."

"I can't," he said hoarsely. "*I* can't. *I* can't tell *you*." And the one thing she understood immediately was that it was the most horrible thing he could conceive with his new knowledge.

She watched him fight, and fought herself: "Maybe I can help, Butcher! There's a way I can go into the brain and find out what it is."

He backed away and shook his head. "*You* mustn't. *You* mustn't do that to *me*. Please."

"Butcher, I w-won't." She was confused. "Th-then I . . . I won't." Confusion hurt. "Butcher . . . I-I won't!" Her adolescent stutter staggered in her mouth.

"I——" he began, breath hard, but becoming softer, "I have been alone and not I for a long time. I must be alone for a little while longer."

"I s-see." Suspicion, very small and easily dealt with, came now. When he had backed away, it entered the space between them. But that was human, too. "Butcher? Can you read my mind?"

He looked surprised. "No. I don't even understand how you can read mine."

"All right. I thought maybe there was something in my head that you might be picking up that makes you afraid of me."

He shook his head.

"That's good. Hell, I wouldn't want somebody prying under my scalp. I think I understand."

"I tell you now," he said, coming toward her again, "I and you are one; but I and you are very different. I have seen a lot you will never know. You know of things that I will never see. You have made me not alone, a little. There is a lot in the brain, my brain, about hurting and running and fighting and, even though I was in Titin, a lot about winning. If you are ever in danger, but a real danger where someone might make a mistake with you, then go into the brain, see what is there. Use whatever you need. I ask you, only, to wait until you have done everything else first."

"I'll wait, Butcher," she said.

He held out his hand. "Come."

She took his hand, avoiding the cock spurs.

"No need to see the stasis currents about the alien ship if it is friendly to the Alliance. You and I will stay together a while."

She walked with her shoulder against his arm. "Friend or enemy," she said as they passed through the twilight, heavy with ghosts. "This whole Invasion—sometimes it seems so stupid. That's something they don't allow you to think back where I come from. Here on Jebel Tarik you more or less avoid the question. I envy you that."

"You are going to Administrative Alliance Headquarters because of the Invasion, yes?"

"That's right. But after I go, don't be surprised if I come back." Steps later she looked up again. "That's another thing I wish I could get straight in my head. The Invaders killed my parents, and the second embargo almost killed me. Two of my Navigators lost their wife to the Invaders. Still,

Ron could wonder about just how right the War Yards were. Nobody likes the Invasion, but it goes on. It's so big I never really thought about trying to get out of it before. It's funny to see a whole bunch of people in their odd, and maybe destructive, way doing just that. Maybe I should simply not bother to go to Headquarters, tell Tarik to turn around and head toward the densest part of the Snap.''

"The Invaders," the Butcher said, almost musingly, "they hurt lots of people, you, me. They hurt me too."

"They did?"

"The brain sick, I told you. Invaders did that."

"What did they do?"

The Butcher shrugged. "First thing I remember is escaping from Nueva-nueva York."

"That's the huge port terminal for the Cancer cluster?"

"That's right."

"The Invaders had captured you?"

He nodded. "And did something. Maybe experiment, maybe torture." He shrugged. "It doesn't matter. I can't remember. But when I escaped, I escaped with nothing: no memory, voice, words, name."

"Perhaps you were a prisoner of war, or maybe even somebody important before they captured you——"

He bent and put his cheek against her lips to stop her talking. When he rose, he smiled, sadly she saw. "There are some things the brain may not know, but it can guess: I was always a thief, a murderer, a criminal. And I was no I. The Invaders caught me once. I escaped. The Alliance caught me later at Titin. I escaped——"

"You *escaped* from Titin?"

He nodded. "I will probably be caught again, because that's what happens to criminals in this universe. And maybe I will escape once more." He shrugged. "Maybe I will not be caught again, though." He looked at her, surprised not at her but at something in himself. "I was no I before, but now there is a reason to stay free. I will not be caught again. There is a reason."

"What is it, Butcher?"

"Because I am," he said softly, "and you are."

V

"You finishing u' your dictionary?" Brass asked.

"Finished it yesterday. This is a poem." She closed the notebook. "We should be at the tip of the Tongue soon. Butcher just told me this morning that the Çiribians have been keeping us company for four days. Brass, do you have any idea what they——"

Magnified by the loudspeakers, Tarik's voice: "Ready Jebel for immediate defense. Repeat, immediate defense."

"What the hell is going on now?" Rydra asked. Around them the commons rose in unified activity. "Look, hunt up the crew and get them down to ejection gates."

"That's where the s'ider-boats leave from?"

"Right." Rydra stood.

"We gonna mix it u' some, Ca'tain?"

"If we have to," Rydra said, and started across the floor.

She beat the crew by a minute and caught the Butcher at the ejection hatch. Jebel's fighting crew hurried along the corridor in ordered confusion.

"What's going on? Did the Çiribians get hostile?"

He shook his head. "Invaders twelve degrees off galactic center."

"This close to Administrative Alliance?"

"Yes. And if Jebel Tarik doesn't attack first, Jebel's had it. They're bigger than Jebel, and Jebel's going to bump right into them."

"Tarik's going to attack them?"

143

"Yes."

"Then come on, let's attack."

"You are going with me?"

"I'm a master strategist, remember?"

"Jebel is in danger," the Butcher said. "This will be a greater battle than you saw before."

"The better to use my talents on, my dear. Is your boat equipped to hold a full crew?"

"Yes. But we use the Navigation and Sensory detail of Jebel by remote control."

"Let's take a crew, anyway, just in case we want to break strategy in a hurry. Is Tarik riding with you this time?"

"No."

Up the hall Slug turned the corner, followed by Brass, the Navigators, the insubstantial figures of the discorporate trio, and the platoon.

The Butcher looked from them to Rydra. "All right. Come inside. Get in, gang!"

She kissed his shoulder because she couldn't reach his cheek; the Butcher opened the ejection hatch, and motioned them on.

Allegra, as she started up the ladder, caught Rydra's arm. "Are we gonna fight this time, Captain?" There was an excited smile on her freckled face.

"There's a good chance. Scared?"

"Yep," Allegra said, still grinning, and scurried into the dark tunnel. Rydra and the Butcher brought up the rear.

"They won't have any trouble with this equipment if they have to take over from remote control, will they?"

"This spider-boat is ten feet shorter than the *Rimbaud*. Things are more cramped in discorporate quarters, but everything else is the same."

Rydra thought: We've worked the sensory details on a forty-foot one-generator sloop; this is a breeze, Captain—Basque.

"The captain's cabin is different," he added. "That's where the weapon controls are. We're going to make some mistakes."

"Moralize later," she said. "We'll fight like hell for Jebel Tarik. But on the chance fighting like hell won't do any good, I want to be able to get out of here. No matter what happens, I've got to get back to Administrative Alliance Headquarters."

"Tarik wanted to know if the Çiribian ship will fight beside us. They're still hanging T-ward."

"They'll probably watch the whole business and not understand what's going on, unless they're directly attacked. If they are, they can pretty well take care of themselves. But I doubt they'll join us in an offensive."

"That's bad," the Butcher said. "Because we'll need help."

"Strategy Workshop. Strategy Workshop," Tarik's voice came over the speaker. "Repeat, Strategy Workshop."

Where language charts had hung in her cabin, a viewing screen—replica of the hundred-foot projection in Jebel's gallery—spread over the wall. Where her console had been were ranged and banked assortments of bomb and vibra-blast controls. "Gross, uncivilized weapons," she commented as she sat down on one of the curved shock-boards where her bubble seat had been. "But effective as hell, I would imagine, if you know what you're doing."

"What?" The Butcher strapped himself beside her.

"I was misquoting the late Weapons Master of Armsedge."

The Butcher nodded. "You see to your crew. I'll go over the check list up here."

She switched on the intercom. "Brass, you wired in place?"

"Right."

"Eye, Ear, Nose?"

"It's dusty down here, Captain. When's the last time they swept out this graveyard?"

"I don't care about the dust. Does everything work?"

"Oh, everything works all right . . ." The sentence ended with a ghostly sneeze.

"*Gesundheit*. Slug, what's happening?"

"All in place, Captain." Then muffled: "Will you put those marbles away!'

"Navigation?"

"We're fine. Mollya is teaching Calli judo. But I'm right here and'll call them soon as something happens."

"Keep alert."

The Butcher bent toward her, stroked her hair, and laughed.

"I like them too," she told him. "I just hope we don't have to use them. One of them is a traitor who's tried to get me twice now. I'd rather not give him a third chance. Though if I have to, I think I can handle him this time."

Tarik's voice over the speaker: "Carpenters gather to face thirty-two degrees off galactic center. Hacksaws at the K-ward gate. Ripsaws make ready at the R-ward gate. Crosscut blades ready at T-ward gate."

The ejectors clicked open. The cabin went black and the view-screen flickered with stars and distant gases. Controls gleamed with red and yellow signal lights along the weapon board. Through the underspeakers the chatter of the crews, back with the Navigation department of Jebel, began.

This is gonna be a rough one. Can you see her, Jehosaphat? She's right in front of me. A big mother.

I just hope she ain't seen us yet. Keep cool, Kippi.

"Drill presses, Bandsaws, and Lathes: make sure your components are oiled and your power-lines plugged in."

"That's us," the Butcher said. His hands leapt in the half-dark among the weapon controls.

What's the three ping-pong balls in the mosquito netting?

Tarik says it's a Çiribian ship.

Long as it's on our side, baby, it's fine with me.

"Power tools commence operations. Hand tools mark out for finishing work."

"Zero," the Butcher whispered. Rydra felt the ship jump. The stars began to move. Ten seconds later she saw the snub-snouted Invader rooting toward them.

"Ugly, isn't it," Rydra said.

"Jebel looks about the same size, only smaller. And when we come home, it will be beautiful. There's no way to enlist the Çiribians' help? Tarik will have to attack the Invader directly at her ports and smash as many as he can, which won't be a lot. Then they'll attack, and if they still outnumber Jebel's spider-boats, and surprise doesn't play heavily on Tarik's side, then that's''—she heard fist strike palm in the darkness—''it.''

''You can't just lob a gross, uncivilized atom bomb at them?''

''They have deflectors that would explode it in Tarik's hands.''

''I'm glad I brought the crew then. We may have to make a quick exit to Administrative Alliance Headquarters.''

''If they let us,'' the Butcher said, grimly. ''What strategies then to win?''

''Tell you soon as the attack starts. I have a method, but if I use it too much I pay high.'' She recalled the illness after the incident with Geoffry Cord.

While Tarik continued to set up formations, the men chatted with Jebel and the spider-boats slipped ahead in the night.

It started so fast she nearly missed it. Five hacksaws had slipped within a hundred yards of the Invader. Simultaneously they blasted at the ejector ports, and red beetles scurried from the sides of the black hog. It took four and a half seconds for the remaining twenty-seven ejectors to open and shoot their first barrage of cruisers. But Rydra was already thinking in Babel-17.

Through her distended time sense she saw they did need help. And the articulation of their need was also the answer.

''Break strategy, Butcher. Follow me with ten ships. My crew is taking over.''

The maddening feeling that her English words took so long on her tongue! The Butcher's request—''Kippi, put hacksaws on trail and leave them there!''—seemed like a tape played at quarter speed. But her crew was already in control of the spider-boat. She hissed their trajectory into the mike.

Brass flung them at right angles to the tide, and for a moment she saw the hacksaws behind her. Now a hairpin turn and they drove behind the first sheet of Invader cruisers.

''Warm their behinds!''

The Butcher's hand hesitated at a weapon. ''Drive them toward Jebel?''

"The hell I will. Fire, sweetheart!"

He fired, and the hacksaws followed suit.

In ten seconds it was clear she was right. Tarik lay R-ward. Ahead were the poached eggs, the mosquito netting, the flimsy, feathery vessel of Çiribia. Çiribia was Alliance, and at least one of the Invaders knew it because he fired at the weird contraption hung up on the sky. Rydra saw the Invader's gun-port cough green fire, but the fire never reached the Çiribians. The Invader cruiser turned into white-hot smoke that blackened and dispersed. Then another cruiser went, then three more, then three more.

"Out of here, Brass!" and they swung up and away.

"What was——" the Butcher started.

"A Çiribian heat ray. But they won't use it unless they're attacked. Part of the treaty signed at the Court in '47. So we make the Invaders attack. Want to do it again?"

Brass' voice over the speaker: "We already are, Ca'tain."

She was thinking in English again, waiting for the nausea to hit, but excitement held it back.

"Butcher," came from Tarik now, "what are you doing?"

"It's working, isn't it?"

"Yes. But you've left a hole in our defenses ten miles across."

"Tell him we'll plug it up in a minute as soon as we drive the next batch through."

Tarik must have heard her. "And what do we do for the next sixty seconds, young lady?"

"Fight like hell." And the next batch of herded cruisers disappeared before the Çiribian heat ray. Then from the underspeakers:

Hey, Butcher, they're out for you.

They got the idea you're spearheading this thing.

Butcher, six on your tail. Shake 'em fast.

"I can dodge them easy, Ca'tain," Brass called up. "They're all on remote control. I've got more freedom."

"One more and we can really put the odds on Tarik's side."

"Tarik outnumbers them already," the Butcher said. "This spider-boat has got to shake those burrs." He called into the mike, "Hacksaws disperse and break up the cruisers behind."

Will do. Hold onto your heads, fellows.

Hey, Butcher, one of them's not giving up.

Tarik said: "I thank you for my hacksaws back, but there's something following you that may be out for a hand-to-hand."

Rydra questioned him with a look.

"Heroes," the Butcher grunted disgustedly. "They'll try to grapple, board, and fight."

"Not with these kids on this ship! Brass, turn around and ram them, or come close enough to make them think we're crazy."

"May break a cou'le ribs . . ." The ship swung and they were flung hard against the straps of the shock-boards.

A youngster's voice through the intercom: "Wheeeee . . ."

On the view-screen the Invader cruiser swerved to the side.

"Good chance if they grapple," the Butcher said. "They don't know there's a full crew aboard. They have no more than two——"

"Watch out, Ca'tain!"

The Invader cruiser filled the screen. *Clunnnggg* sang the bones of the spider-boat.

The Butcher yanked at the straps of the shock-board and grinned. "Now to fighting hand-to-hand. Where are *you* going?"

"With you."

"You have a vibra-gun?" He tightened the holster on his stomach.

"Sure do." She pushed aside a panel of her loose blouse. "And this, too. Vanadium wire, six inches. Wicked thing."

"Come." He slapped the lever on a gravity inductor down to full field.

"What's that for?"

They were already in the corridor.

"To fight in a space suit out there is no good. False gravity field released around both ships will keep a breatheable atmosphere to about twenty feet from the surface and keep some heat in . . . more or less.''

''What's less?'' She swung behind him into the lift.

''It's about ten degrees below zero out there.''

He had abandoned even his breech since the evening they had met in Jebel's graveyard. All he wore was the holster. ''I guess we won't be out there long enough to need overcoats.''

''I guarantee you, whoever is out there more than a minute will be dead, and not from overexposure.'' His voice suddenly deepened as they ducked into the hatchway. ''If you don't know what you're doing, stay back.'' Then he bent to brush her cheek with amber hair. ''But you know, and I know. We must do it well.''

In the same motion that he raised his head, he released the hatch. Cold came in for them. She didn't feel it. The increased metabolic rate that accompanied Babel-17 wrapped her in a shield of physical indifference. Something went flying overhead. They knew what to do and both did it; they ducked. Whatever it was exploded—the explosion identifying it as a grenade that had just missed coming into the hatch—and light bleached the Butcher's face. He leaped and the fading glow slid down his body.

She followed him, reassured by the slow motion effect of Babel-17. She spun as she jumped. Someone ducked behind the ten foot bulge of an outrigger. She fired at him, the slow motion giving her time to take careful aim. She didn't wait to see if she hit, but kept turning. The Butcher was making for the ten foot wide column of the Invader's grapple.

Like a triple clawed crab, the enemy boat angled away into the night. K-ward rose the flattened spiral of the home galaxy. Shadows were carbon-paper black on the smooth hulls. From the K-ward side nobody could see her, unless her movement blotted a fugitive star or passed into the direct light of Specelli arm itself.

She jumped again—at the surface of the Invader cruiser now. For a moment it got much colder. Then she struck, near the grappler base, and rolled to her knees as, below, someone heaved another grenade at the hatch. They hadn't realized she and the Butcher were out yet. Good. She fired. And another hiss sounded from where the Butcher must be.

In the darkness below, figures moved. Then a vibra-blast stung the metal hatch beneath her hand. It came from her own ship's hatch and she wasted a quarter of a second analyzing and disregarding the idea that the spy she had been afraid of from her own crew had joined the Invaders. Rather, the Invader's tactic had been to keep them from leaving their ship and blow them up in the hatch. It had failed, so now they had taken cover in the hatch itself for safety and were firing from there. She fired, fired again. From his hiding place behind the other grapple, the Butcher was doing the same.

A section of the hatch rim began to glow from the repeated blasts. Then a familiar voice was calling, "All right, all right already, Butcher! You got them, Ca'tain!"

Rydra monkeyed down the grapple, as Brass turned the hatch light on and stood up in the glow that fanned across the bulkhead. The Butcher, gun down, came from his hiding place.

The underlighting distorted Brass' demon features still further. He held a limp figure in each claw.

"Actually this one's mine." He shook the right one, "He was trying to crawl back into the shi', so I ste''ed on his head." The pilot heaved the limp bodies onto the hullplates. "I don't know about you folks, but I'm cold. Reason I came up here in the first 'lace was Diavalo told me to tell you when you were ready for a coffee break, he'd fixed u' some Irish whiskey. Or maybe you'd 'refer hot buttered rum? Come on, come on! You're blue!"

At the lift her mind got back to English and she began to shiver. The frost on the Butcher's hair had started to melt to shiny droplets along his hairline. Her hand stung where she had just missed a burning.

"Hey," she said, as they stepped into the corridor, "if you're up here, Brass, who's watching the store?"

"Ki''i. We went back on remote control."

"Rum," the Butcher said. "No butter and not hot. Just rum."

"Man after my own heart," nodded Brass. He dropped

one arm around Rydra's shoulder, the other around the Butcher's. Friendly, but also, she realized, he was half-carrying both of them.

Something went *clang* through the ship.

The pilot glanced at the ceiling. "Maintenance just cut those grapples loose." He edged them into the captain's cabin. As they collapsed on the shock-boards, he called into the intercom: "Hey, Diavalo, come u' here and get these 'eo'le drunk, huh? They deserve it."

"Brass!" She caught his arm as he started back out. "Can you get us from here to Administrative Alliance Headquarters?"

He scratched his ear. "We're right at the ti' of the Tongue. I only know the inside of the Sna' by chart. But Sensory tells me we're right in something that must be the beginning of Natal-beta Current. I know it flows out of the Sna' and we can take it down to Atlas-run and then into Administrative Alliance's front door. We're about eighteen, twenty hours away."

"Let's go." She looked at the Butcher. He made no objection.

"Good idea," Brass said. "About half of Tarik is . . . eh, discor'orate."

"The Invaders won?"

"No'e. The Çiribians finally got the idea, roasted that big 'ig, and took off. But only after Tarik got a hole in its side large enough to 'ut three s'ider-boats through, sideways. Ki''i tells me everyone who's still alive is sealed off in one quarter of the shi', but they have no running 'ower."

"What about Tarik?" the Butcher asked.

"Dead," Brass said.

Diavalo poked his white head down the entrance hatch. "Here you go."

Brass took the bottle and the glasses.

Then static on the speaker: "Butcher, we just saw you cast off the Invaders' cruiser. So, you got out alive."

Butcher leaned forward and picked up the mike. "Butcher alive, chief."

"Some people have all the luck. Captain Wong, I expect you to write me an elegy."

"Tarik?" She sat down next to the Butcher. "We're going to Administrative Alliance Headquarters now. We'll come back with help."

"At your convenience, Captain. We're just a trifle crowded, though."

"We're leaving now."

Brass was already out the door.

"Slug, are the kids all right?"

"Present and accounted for. Captain, you didn't give anyone permission to bring firecrackers aboard, did you?"

"Not that I remember."

"That's all I wanted to know. Ratt, come back here . . ."

Rydra laughed. "Navigation?"

"Ready when you are," Ron said. In the background she heard Mollya's voice: *"Nilitaka kulala, nilale milele——"*

"You can't go to sleep forever," Rydra said. "We're taking off!"

"Mollya's teaching us a poem in Swahili," Ron explained.

"Oh. Sensory?"

"Ka*chuuu*! I always said, Captain, keep your graveyard clean. You might need it some day. Tarik's a case in point. We're ready."

"Get Slug to send one of the kids down with a dust mop. All wired in, Brass?"

"Checked out and ready, Ca'tain."

The stasis generators cut in and she leaned back on the shock-board. Inside something at last relaxed. "I didn't think we were going to get out of there." She turned to the Butcher, who sat on the edge of his board watching her. "You know I'm nervous as a cat. And I don't feel too well. Oh, hell, it's starting." With the relaxation the sickness which she had put off for so long began to climb her body. "This whole thing makes me feel like I'm about to fly apart. You know when you doubt everything, mistrust all your feelings, I begin to think I'm not me anymore . . ." Her breath got painful in her throat.

"I am," he said softly, "and you are."

"Don't ever let me doubt it, Butcher. But I even have to wonder about that. There's a spy among my crew. I told you that, didn't I? Maybe it's Brass and he's going to hurl us into another nova!'' Within the sickness was a blister of hysteria. The blister broke, and she smacked the bottle from the Butcher's hand. "Don't drink that! D-D-Diavalo, he might poison us!" She rose unsteadily. There was a red haze over everything. ". . . Or one of the d-d-dead. How . . . how can I f-f-f . . . fight a ghost?" Then pain hit her stomach, and she staggered back as away from a blow. Fear came with the pain. The emotions were moving behind his face, and even they blurred in her attempt to see them clearly. ". . . to kill . . . k-k-kill *us*!" she whispered, ". . . s-s-something to kill . . . s-s-so no y-*you*, n-n-no *I* . . ."

It was to get away from the pain which meant danger and the danger which meant silence that she did it. He had said, *If you are ever in danger . . . then go into my brain, see what is there, and use what you need.*

An image in her mind without words: once she, Muels, and Fobo had been in a barroom brawl on Tantor. She had caught a punch in the jaw and staggered back, shocked and turning, just as somebody picked the bar mirror from behind the counter and flung it at her. Her own terrified face had come screaming toward her, smashed over her outstretched hand. As she stared at the Butcher's face, through pain and Babel-17, it happened all over—

PART FOUR

~~~~~~

The Butcher

. . . *turning in the brain to wake*
with wires behind his eyes, forking the joints
akimbo. He wakes, wired,
forked fingers crackling, gagging on his tongue.
We wake, turning.
     Spined against the floor,
his spine turning, chest hollowed,
air in the wires, sparks
glint from the wired ceiling, tapping
his sparking fingernails. Coughs, cries.
The twin behind the eyes coughs, cries.
The dark twin doubles on the floor, swallows his tongue.
Splashed to the dark pole circuited behind
the eyes, the dark twin snaps his spine free, slaps
his palms against the ceiling. Charged beads fly.
The ceiling, polarized, batters his cheek with metal.
Tears free skin. Tears ribs,
torn pectorals off metal curved away
black, behind the cracks, dried,
that are his torn lips. More.

Buttocks and shoulderblades grind on the floor
gritty and green with brine.
    They wake.
We wake, turning.
    He, gargling blood, turns,
born, on the wet floor . . .

                    —from *The Dark Twin*

1

~~~~~~

"We just left the Sna', Ca'tain. You two drunk yet?"

Rydra's voice: "No."

"How do you like that. I guess you're all right, though."

Rydra's voice: "The brain fine. The body fine."

"Huh? Hey, Butcher, she didn't have one of her s'ells again?"

The Butcher's voice: "No."

"Both of you sound funny as hell. Shall I send the Slug u' there to take a look at you?"

The Butcher's voice: "No."

"All right. It's clear sailing now, and I can 'ut a cou'le of hours off. What do you say?"

The Butcher's voice: "What is to say?"

"Try 'thanks'. You know, I'm flying my tail off down here."

Rydra's voice: "Thanks."

"You're welcome, I guess. I'll leave you two alone. Hey, I'm sorry if I interru'ted something."

Butcher, I didn't know! I couldn't have known!

And in the echo their minds fused a cry, Couldn't have—couldn't. This light—

I told Brass, told him you must speak a language without the word 'I' and I said I didn't know of one; but there was one, the obvious one, Babel-17 . . . !

Congruent synapses quivered sympathetically till images locked, and out of herself she created, saw him—

—In the solitary confinement box of Titin, he scratched a map on the green wall paint with his spur over the palimpsestic obscenities of two centuries' prisoners, a map that they would follow on his escape and would take them in the wrong direction; she watched him pace that four-foot space for three months till his six and a half-foot frame was starved to a hundred and one pounds and he collapsed in the chains of starvation.

On a triple rope of words she climbed from the pit: starve, stave, stake; collapse, collate, collect; chains, change, chance.

He collected his winnings from the cashier and was about to stride across the maroon carpet of *Casino Cosmica* to the door when the black croupier blocked his way, smiling at the thick money case. "Would you like to take one more chance, sir? Something to challenge a player of your skill?" He was taken to a magnificent 3-D chessboard with glazed ceramic pieces. "You play against the house computer. Against each piece you lose, you stake a thousand credits. Each piece you win gains you the same. Checks win or lose you five hundred. Checkmate gains the winner one hundred times the rest of the game's earnings, for either you or the house.'' It was a game to even out his exorbitant winnings—and he had been winning exorbitantly. "Going home and take this money now," he said to the croupier. The croupier smiled and said, "The house insists you play.'' She watched, fascinated, while the Butcher shrugged, turned to the board—and checkmated the computer in a seven move fool's mate. They gave him his million credits—and tried to kill him three times before he got to the mouth of the casino. They did not succeed, but the sport was better than the gambling.

Watching him function and react in these situations, her mind shook inside his, curving to his pain or pleasure, strange emotions because they were ego-less and inarticulate, magic, seductive, mythical. *Butcher—*

She managed to interrupt the headlong circling.

—if you understood Babel-17 all along, her questions hurled in her own storming brain, *why did you only use it gratuitously for yourself, an evening of gambling, a bank robbery, when a day later you would lose everything and make no attempt to keep things for yourself?*

What "self"? There was no "I".

She had entered him in some bewildering reversed sexuality. Enclosing her, he was in agony. *The light—you make! You make!* his crying in terror.

Butcher, she asked, more familiar in patterning words about emotional turbulences than he, *what does my mind in yours look like?*

Bright, bright moving, he howled, the analytical precision of Babel-17, crude as stone to articulate their melding, making so many patterns, reforming them.

That's just being a poet, she explained, the oblique connection momentarily cutting the flood through. *Poet in Greek means maker or builder.*

There's one! There's a pattern now. Ahhhh!—so bright, bright!

Just that simple semantic connection? She was astounded.

But the Greeks were poets three thousand years ago and you are a poet now. You snatch words together over such distance and their wakes blind me. Your thoughts are all fire,

*over shapes I cannot catch. They sound like music too deep,
that shakes me.*

*That's because you were never shaken before. But I'm
flattered.*

*You are so big inside me I will break. I see the pattern
named* The Criminal *and artistic consciousness meeting in the
same head with one language between them . . .*

Yes, I had started to think something like—

Flanking it, shapes called Baudelaire—*Ahhh!—and* Villon.
They were ancient French po—

*Too bright! Too bright! The "I" in me is not strong
enough to hold them. Rydra, when I look at the night and
stars, it is only a passive act, but you are active even
watching, and halo the stars with more luminous flame.*

What you perceive you change, Butcher. But you must
perceive it.

*I must—the light; central in you I see mirror and motion
fused, and the pictures are meshed, rotating, and everything
is choice.*

My poems! It was the embarrassment of nakedness.

Definitions of "I" each great and precise.

She thought: I/Aye/Eye, the self, a sailor's *yes*, the organ
of visual perception.

He began, *You—*

You/Ewe/Yew, the other self, a female sheep, the Celtic
vegetative symbol for death.

*—you ignite my words with meanings I can only glimpse.
What am I surrounding? What am I, surrounding you?*

Still watching, she saw him commit robbery, murder,
mayhem, because the semantic validity of *mine* and *thine*
were ruined in a snarl of frayed synapses. *Butcher, I heard it
ringing in your muscles, that loneliness, that made you
make Tarik hook up the* Rimbaud *just to have someone near
you who could speak this analytical tongue, the same reason
you tried to save the baby,* she whispered.

Images locked on her brain.

Long grass whispered by the weir. Alleppo's moons
fogged the evening. The plainsmobile hummed, and with
measured impatience he flicked the ruby emblem on the
steering wheel with the tip of his left spur. Lill twisted against

him, laughing. "You know, Butcher, if Mr. Big thought you'd driven out here with me on such a romantic night he'd get very hostile. You're really gonna take me to Paris when you finish here?" Unnamed warmth mixed in him with unnamed impatience. Her shoulder was damp under his hand, her lips red. She had coiled her champagne colored hair high over one ear. Her body beside his moved in a rippling motion that had the excuse of her turning to face him. "If you're kidding me, about Paris, I'll tell Mr. Big. If I were a smart girl, I'd wait till after you took me there before I let us get . . . friendly." Her breath was perfumed in the sweltering night. He moved his other hand up her arm. "Butcher, get me off this hot, dead world. Swamps, caves, rain! Mr. Big scares me, Butcher! Take me away from him, to Paris. Don't just be pretending. I want to go with you so bad." She made another laughing sound with only her lips. "I guess I'm . . . I'm not a smart girl after all." He placed his mouth against her mouth—and broke her neck with one thrust of his hands. Her eyes still open, she sagged backwards. The hypodermic ampule she had been about to plunge into his shoulder fell from her hand, rolled across the dashboard, and dropped among the foot pedals. He carried her into the weir, and came back muddy to mid-thigh. In the seat he flipped on the radio. "It's finished, Mr. Big."

"Very good. I was listening. You can pick up your money in the morning. It was very silly of her to try and double cross me out of that fifty thousand."

The plainsmobile was rolling, the warm breeze drying the mud on his arms, the long grass hissing against the runners.

Butcher . . . !

But that's me, Rydra.

I know. But I . . .

I had to do the same thing to Mr. Big himself two weeks later.

Where did you promise to take him?

The gambling caves of Minos. And once I had to crouch—

—though it was his body crouching under the green light of Kreto, breathing with wide open mouth to stop all sound, it was her anticipation, her fear controlled to calm. The loader

in his red uniform halts and wipes his forehead with a
bandanna. Step out quickly, taps his shoulder. The loader
turns, surprised, and the hands come up leading with the
heel, cock spurs opening the loader's belly, which spills all
over the platform, and then running, while the alarms start,
vaulting the sandbags, snatching up the hawser chain and
swinging it down on the amazed face of the guard standing on
the other side who turned to see him with arms surprised
open—

—broke into the open and got away, he told her. *The trail
disguise worked and the Tracers couldn't follow me past the
lava pits.*

*Opening you up, Butcher. All the running, opening me?
Does it hurt, does it help? I didn't know.*

*But there were no words in your mind. Even Babel-17
was like the brain noise of a computer engaged in a purely
synaptical analysis.*

Yes. Now do you begin to understand—

—standing, shivering in the roaring caves of Dis where
he had been wombed nine months, eaten all the food,
Lonny's pet dog, then Lonny who had frozen to death trying
to climb over the mounded ice—till suddenly the planetoid
swung out from the shadow of Cyclops and blazing Ceres
flared in the sky so that in forty minutes the cave was flooded
with ice water to his waist. When he finally freed his
hop-sled, the water was warm and he was slimy with sweat.
He ran at top speed for the two mile twilight strip, setting the
automatic pilot a moment before he collapsed, dizzy with
heat. He fainted two minutes before he pulled into Gotter-
dammerung.

*Faint in the darkness of your lost memory, Butcher, I
must find you. Who were you before Nueva-nueva York?*

And he turned to her in gentleness. *You're afraid, Rydra?
Like before . . .*

*No, not like before. You're teaching me something, and
it's shaking my whole picture of the world and myself. I
thought I was afraid before because I couldn't do what you
could do, Butcher.* The white flame went blue, protective, and
trembled. *But I was afraid because I could do all those
things, and for my own reasons, not your lack of reasons,*

because I am, and you are. I'm a lot bigger than I thought I was, Butcher, and I don't know whether to thank you or damn you for showing me. And something inside was crying, stuttering, was still. She turned in the silences she had taken from him, fearfully, and in the silences something waited for her to speak, alone, for the first time.

Look at yourself, Rydra.

Mirrored in him, she saw growing in the light of her, a darkness without words, only noise—growing! And cried out at its name and shape. The broken circuit boards! *Butcher, those tapes that could only have been made on my console when I was there! Of course—!*

Rydra, we can control them if we can name them.

How can we, now? We have to name ourselves first. And you don't know who you are.

Your words, Rydra, can we somehow use your words to find out who I am?

Not my words, Butcher. But maybe yours, maybe Babel-17. No . . .

I am, she whispered, *believe me, Butcher, and you are.*

III

"Headquarters, Captain. Take a look through the sensory helmet. Those radio nets look like fireworks, and corporate souls tell me it smells like cornedbeef hash and fried eggs. Hey, thanks for getting us dusted out. Had a tendency toward hayfever when I was alive that I never did shake."

Rydra's voice: "The crew will debark with the Captain and the Butcher. The crew will take them to General Forester, together, and not let them be separated."

The Butcher's voice: "There is a tape recording in the Captain's cabin on the console containing a grammar of Babel-17. The Slug will send that tape immediately to Dr.

Markus T'mwarba on Earth by special delivery. Then inform Dr. T'mwarba by stellarphone that the tape was sent, at what time, and its contents.''

"Brass, Slug! Something's wrong up there!" Ron's voice overcut the Captain's signal. "You ever heard them talk like that? Hey, Captain Wong, what's the matter . . . ?"

PART FIVE

Markus T'mwarba

Growing older I descend November.
The asymptotic cycle of the year
plummets to now. In crystal reveries
I pass beneath a fixed white line of trees
where dry leaves lie for footsteps to dismember.
They crackle with a muted sound like fear.
That and the wind is all that I can hear.
I ask cold air, "What is the word that frees?"
The wind says, "Change," and the white sun, "Remember."

—from *Electra*

1

~~~~~~

The spool of tape, the imperative directive from General
Forester, and the infuriated Dr. T'mwarba reached Danil D.
Appleby's office within thirty seconds of each other.

He was opening the flat box when the noise outside the
partition made him look up. "Michael," he asked the intercom. "What's that?"

"Some madman who says he's a psychiatrist!"

"I am not mad!" Dr. T'mwarba said loudly. "But I
know how long it takes a package to get from Administrative
Alliance Headquarters to Earth, and it should have reached
my door with this morning's mail. It didn't, which means it's
been held up, and this is where you do things like that. Let me
in."

Then the door crashed back against the wall and he was.

Michael craned around T'mwarba's hip: "Hey, Dan, I'm
sorry. I'll call the——"

Dr. T'mwarba pointed to the desk and said, "That's
mine. Gimme."

"Don't bother, Michael," the Customs Officer said
before the door was slammed again. "Good afternoon, Dr.
T'mwarba. Won't you sit down. This is addressed to you,
isn't it? Don't look so surprised that I know you. I also handle
security psyche-index integration, and all of us in the department know your brilliant work in schizoid-differentiation. I'm
so glad to meet you."

"Why can't I have my package?"

"One moment and I'll find out." As he picked up the

directive, Dr. T'mwarba picked up the box and stuck it in his pocket:

"Now you can explain."

The Customs Officer opened the letter. "It seems," he said, pressing his knee against the desk to release some of the hostility that had built up in very little time, "that you may have . . . eh, keep the tape on condition you leave for Administrative Alliance Headquarters this evening on the *Midnight Falcon* and bring the tape with you. Passage has been booked, thanking you in advance for your cooperation, sincerely, General X. J. Forester."

"Why?"

"He doesn't say. I'm afraid, doctor, that unless you agree to go, I won't be able to let you keep that. And we can get it back."

"That's what you think. Have you any idea what they want?"

The officer shrugged. "You were expecting it. Who's it from?"

"Rydra Wong."

"Wong?" The Customs Officer had put both knees against the desk. He dropped them. "The poet, Rydra Wong? You know Rydra, too?"

"I've been her psychiatric advisor since she was twelve. Who are you?"

"I'm Danil D. Appleby. Had I known you were Rydra's friend, I would have ushered you up here myself!" The hostility had acted as a take off from which to spring into ebullient camaraderie. "If you're leaving on the *Falcon,* you've got time to step out a little while with me, haven't you? I was going to leave work early anyway. I have to stop off at . . . well, someplace in Transport Town. Why didn't you say you knew her before? There's a delightfully ethnic place right near where I'm going. Get a reasonable meal and a good drink there; do you follow the wrestling? Most people think it's illegal, but you can watch it there. Ruby and Python are on display this evening. If you'll just make that one stop with me first, I know you'll find it fascinating. And I'll get you to the *Falcon* on time."

"I think I know the place."

"You go downstairs and they have this big bubble on the ceiling, where they fight . . . ?" Effervescent, he leaned forward. "As a matter of fact, Rydra first took me there."

Dr. T'mwarba began to smile.

The Customs Officer slapped the desk top. "We had a wild time that night! Simply wild!" He narrowed his eyes. "Ever been picked up by one of those . . ." He snapped his fingers three times. ". . . in the discorporate sector? Now that still *is* illegal. But take a walk out there some evening."

"Come," laughed the doctor. "Dinner and a drink; best idea I've heard all day. I'm starved and I haven't seen a good match in four months."

"I've never been inside *this* place before," the Officer said, as they stepped from the monorail. "I called to make an appointment but they told me I didn't need one, just to come in; they were open till six. I figured what the hell, I'd take off from work." They crossed the street and passed the newsstand where frayed, unshaven loaders were picking up schedule sheets for incoming flights. Three stellarmen in green uniforms lurched along the sidewalk, arms about each other's shoulders. "You know," the Customs Officer was saying, "I've had quite a battle with myself; I've wanted to do it ever since I first came down here—hell, ever since I first went to the movies and saw pictures. But anything really bizarre just wouldn't go at the office. Then I said to myself, it could be something simple, covered up when I was wearing clothes. Here we are."

The Officer pushed open the door of Plastiplasm Plus ("Addendums, Superscripts, and Footnotes to the Beautiful Body").

"You know I always meant to ask someone who was an authority; do you think there's anything psychologically off about wanting something like this?"

"Not at all."

A young lady with blue eyes, lips, hair and wings said, 'You can go right in. Unless you want to check our catalogue irst."

"Oh, I know exactly what I want," the Customs Officer assured her. "This way?"

"That's right."

"Actually," Dr. T'mwarba went on, "it's psychologically important to feel in control of your body, that you can change it, shape it. Going on a six month diet or a successful muscle building program can give quite a sense of satisfaction. So can a new nose, chin, or set of scales and feathers."

They were in a room with white operating tables. "Can I help you?" asked a smiling, Polynesian cosmetisurgeon in a blue smock. "Why don't you lie down here?"

"I'm just watching," Dr. T'mwarba said.

"It's listed in your catalogue as 5463," the Customs Officer declared. "I want it there." He clapped his left hand to his right shoulder.

"Oh yes. I rather like that one myself. Just a moment." He opened the top of a stand by the table. Instruments glittered.

The surgeon went off to the glass-faced refrigeration unit at the far wall where behind the glass doors intricate plastiplasm shapes were blurred by frost. He returned with a tray full of various fragments. The only recognizable one was the front half of a miniature dragon with jeweled eyes, glittering scales, and opalescent wings: it was less than two inches long.

"When he's connected up to your nervous system, you'll be able to make him whistle, hiss, roar, flap his wings and spit sparks, though it may take a few days to assimilate him into your body picture. Don't be surprised if at first he just burps and looks seasick. Take your shirt off, please."

The Officer opened his collar.

"We'll just block off all sensation from your shoulder on . . . there, that didn't really hurt. This? Oh, it's a local venal and arterial constrictant; we want to keep things clean. Now, we'll just cut you along the —well, if it upsets you, don't look. Talk to your friend there. It'll just take a few minutes. Oh, that must have tickled all down in your tummy. Never mind. Just once more. Fine. That's your shoulder joint. I know; your arm does look sort of funny hanging there without it. We'll just stick in this transparent plastiplasm cage now. Exact same articulation as your shoulder joint, and it holds your muscles out of the way. See, it's got grooves for your arteries. Move your chin, please. If you want to watch, look in the mirror. Now we'll just crimp it around the edges. Keep this vivatape around the rim of the cage for a couple of days until things grow together. There's not much chance of its pulling apart unless you strain your arm suddenly, but you ought to be safe. Now I'll just connect the little fellow in there to the nerve. This will hurt——''

"Gnnnnn!" The Customs Officer half rose.

"—Sit! Sit! All right, the little catch here—look in the mirror—is to open the cage. You'll learn how to make him come out and do tricks, but don't be impatient. It takes a bit of time. Let me turn the feeling back on in your arm."

The surgeon removed the electrodes and the Officer whistled.

"Stings a little. It will for about an hour. If there's any redness or inflammation, please don't hesitate to come back. Everything that comes through that doorway gets perfectly sterilized, but every five or six years somebody comes down with an infection. You can put your shirt on now."

As they walked into the street, the Customs Officer flexed his shoulder. "You know they claim it should make absolutely no difference." He made a face. "My fingers feel funny. Do you think he might have bruised a nerve?"

'I doubt it," Dr. T'mwarba said, "but you will if you keep twisting like that. You'll pull the vivatape loose. Let's go eat."

The Officer fingered his shoulder. "It feels odd to have a three inch hole there and your arm still working."

"So," Dr. T'mwarba said over his mug, "Rydra first brought you to Transport Town."

"Yes. Actually—well, I only met her that once. She was getting a crew together for a government sponsored trip. I was just along to approve indices. But something happened that evening."

"What was it?"

"I saw a bunch of the weirdest, oddest people I had ever met in my life, who thought different, and acted different, and even made love different. And they made me laugh, and get angry, and be happy, and be sad, and excited, and even fall in love a little myself.'' He glanced up at the sphere of the wrestling arena aloft in the bar. ''And they didn't seem to be so weird or strange anymore.''

''Communication was working that night?''

''I guess so. It's presumptuous my calling her by her first name. But I feel like she's my . . . friend. I'm a lonely man, in a city of lonely men. And when you find some place where—communications are working, you come back to see if it will happen again.''

''Has it?''

Danil D. Appleby looked down from the ceiling and began to unbutton his shirt. ''Let's have dinner.'' He shrugged his shirt over the back of the chair and glanced down at the dragon caged in his shoulder. ''You come back anyway.'' Turning in his seat, he picked his shirt up, folded it neatly, and put it down again. ''Dr. T'mwarba, have you any idea why they want you to come to Administrative Alliance Headquarters?''

''I assume it concerns Rydra and this tape.''

''Because you said you were her doctor. I just hope it isn't a medical reason. If anything happened to her, it would be terrible. For me, I mean. She managed to say so much to me in that one evening, so very simply.'' He laughed and ran his finger around the rim of the cage. The beast inside gurgled. ''And half the time she wasn't even looking in my direction when she said it.''

''I hope she's all right,'' Dr. T'mwarba said. ''She'd better be.''

II

Before the *Midnight Falcon* landed, he inveigled the captain into letting him speak with Flight Control. ''I want to know when the *Rimbaud* came in.''

"Just a moment, sir. I don't believe it has. Certainly not within the past six months. It would take a little time to check back further than——"

"No. It would be more like the past few days. Are you sure the *Rimbaud* did not land here recently under Captain Rydra Wong?"

"Wong? I believe she did land yesterday, but not in the *Rimbaud*. It was an unmarked fighter ship. There was some mixup because the serial numbers had been filed off the tubes and there was a possibility it might have been stolen."

"Was Captain Wong all right when she disembarked?"

"She'd apparently relinquished command to her——" The voice stopped.

"Well?"

"Excuse me, sir. This has been all marked classified. I didn't see the sticker, and it was accidentally put back in the regular file. I can't give you any more information. It's only cleared to authorized persons."

"I'm Dr. Markus T'mwarba," the doctor said, with authority and no idea whether it would do any good.

"Oh, there is a notation concerning you, sir. But you're not on the cleared list."

"Then what the hell does it say, young lady?"

"Just that if you requested information, to refer you directly to General Forester."

An hour later he walked into General Forester's office. "All right, what's the matter with Rydra?"

"Where's the tape?"

"If Rydra wanted me to have it, she had good reason. If she'd wanted you to have it, she would have given it to you. Believe me, you won't get your hands on it unless I give it to you."

"I'd expected more cooperation, Doctor."

"I am cooperating. I'm here, General. But you must want me to do something, and unless I know exactly what's going on, I can't."

"It's a very unmilitary attitude," General Forester said, coming around the desk. "It's one I'm having to deal with more and more, recently. I don't know whether I like it. But I

don't know whether I dislike it either." The green-suited
stellarman sat on the desk's edge, touched the stars on his
collar, looked pensive. "Miss Wong was the first person I've
met in a long time to whom I could not say: do this, do that,
and be damned if you inquire about the consequences. The
first time I spoke to her about Babel-17, I thought I could just
hand her the transcription, and she would hand it back to me
in English. She told me flatly: No; I would have to tell her
more. That's the first time anyone's told me I *had* to do
anything in fourteen years. I may not like it; I sure as hell
respect it." His hands dropped protectively to his lap. (Protective? Was it Rydra who had taught him to interpret that
movement, T'mwarba wondered briefly.) "It's so easy to get
caught in your fragment of the world. When a voice comes
cutting through, it's important. Rydra Wong . . ." and the
General stopped, an expression settling on his features that
made T'mwarba chill as he looked at it with what Rydra had
taught him.

"Is she all right, General Forester? Is this something
medical?"

"I don't know," the General said. "There's a woman in
my inner office—and a man. I can't tell you whether the
woman is Rydra Wong or not. It certainly isn't the same
woman I talked to that evening on Earth about Babel-17."

But T'mwarba, already at the door, shoved it open.

A man and a woman looked up. The man was massively
graceful, amber-haired—a convict, the doctor realized from the
mark on his arm. The woman—

He put both fists on his hips: "All right, what am I about
to say to you?"

She said: "Non comprehension."

Breathing pattern, curl of hands in lap, carriage of
shoulders, the details whose import she had demonstrated to
him a thousand times: he learned in the horrifying length of a
breath just how much they identified. For a moment he
wished she had never taught him, because they were all gone,
and their absence in her familiar body were worse than scars
and disfigurements. He began in a voice that was habitually
for her, the one he had praised or chastened her with, "I was
going to say—if this is a joke, sweetheart, I'll . . . paddle

you." It ended with the voice for strangers, for salesmen and wrong numbers, and he felt unsteadied. "If you're not Rydra, who are you?"

She said: "Non comprehension of the question. General Forester, is this man Doctor Markus T'mwarba?"

"Yes, he is."

"Look." Dr. T'mwarba turned to the General. "I'm sure you've gone over fingerprints, metabolic rates, retina patterns, that sort of identification."

"That's Rydra Wong's body, Doctor."

"All right: hypnotics, experiential imprinting, graft of presynapsed cortical matter—can you think of any other way to get one mind into another head?"

"Yes. Seventeen. There's no evidence of any of them." The General stepped from the door. "She's made it clear she wants to speak to you alone. I'll be right outside." He closed the door.

"I'm pretty sure who you're not," Doctor T'mwarba said after a moment.

The woman blinked and said: "Message from Rydra Wong, delivered verbatim, non comprehension of its significance." Suddenly the face took on its familiar animation. Her hands grasped each other, and she leaned slightly forward: "Mocky, am I glad you got here. I can't sustain this very long, so here goes. Babel-17 is more or less like Onoff, Algol, Fortran. I am telepathic after all, only I've just learned how to control it. I . . . we've taken care of the Babel-17 sabotage attempts. Only we're prisoners, and if you want to get us out, forget about who I am. Use what's on the end of the tape, and find out who he is!" She pointed to the Butcher.

The animation left, the rigidity returned to her face. The whole transformation left T'mwarba holding his breath. He shook his head, started breathing again. After a moment he went back into the General's office. "Who's the jailbird?" he asked matter-of-factly.

"We're tracking that down now. I hoped to have the report this morning." Something on the desk flashed. "Here it is now." He flipped up a slot in the desk top and pulled out a folder. As he slit the seal, he paused. "Would you like to tell me what Onoff, Algol, and Fortran are?"

"To be sure, listening at keyholes." T'mwarba sighed and sat down in a bubble chair in front of the desk. "They're ancient, twentieth century languages—artificial languages that were used to program computers, designed especially for machines. Onoff was the simplest. It reduced everything to a combination of two words, *on* and *off*, or the binary number system. The others were more, complicated."

The General nodded, and finished opening the folder. "That guy came from the swiped spider-boat with her. The crew got very upset when we wanted to put them in separate quarters." He shrugged. "It's something psychic. Why take chances? We leave them together."

"Where is the crew? Were they able to help you?"

"Them? It's like trying to talk to something out of your bad dreams. Transport. Who can talk to people like that?"

"Rydra could," Doctor T'mwarba said. "I'd like to see if I might."

"If you wish. We're keeping them at Headquarters." He opened the folder, then made a face. "Odd. There's a fairly detailed account of his existence for a five year period that started with some petty thievery, strong arm work, then graduates to a couple of rub-outs. A bank robbery——" The General pursed his lips and nodded appreciatively. "He served two years in the penal caves of Titin, escaped—this boy *is* something. Disappeared into the Specelli Snap where he either died, or perhaps got into a shadow-ship. He certainly didn't die. But before December '61, he doesn't seem to have existed. He's usually called the Butcher."

Suddenly the General dived into a drawer and came up with another folder. "Kreto, Earth, Minos, Callisto," he read, then slapped the folder with the back of his hand. "Aleppo, Rhea, Olympia, Paradise, Dis!"

"What's that, the Butcher's itinerary until he went into Titin?"

"It just so happens it is. But it's also the locations of a series of accidents that began in December '61. We'd just gotten around to connecting them up with Babel-17. We'd only been working with recent 'accidents', but then this pattern from a few years ago turned up. Reports of the same sort of radio exchange. Do you think Miss Wong has brought home our saboteur?''

"Could be. Only that isn't Rydra in there."

"Well, yes. I guess you could say that."

"For similar reasons I would gather that the gentleman with her is not the Butcher."

"Who do you think he is?"

"Right now I don't know. I'd say it's fairly important we found out." He stood up. "Where can I get hold of Rydra's crew?"

III

"A pretty snazzy place!" Calli said as they stepped from the lift at the top floor of Alliance Towers.

"Nice now," said Mollya, "to be able to walk about."

A headwaiter in white formal wear came across the civet rug, looked just a trifle askance at Brass, then said, "This is your party, Dr. T'mwarba?"

"That's right. We have an alcove by the window. You can bring us a round of drinks right away. I've ordered already."

The waiter nodded, turned, and led them toward a high, arched window that looked over Alliance Plaza. A few people turned to watch them.

"Administrative Headquarters can be a very pleasant place." Dr. T'mwarba smiled.

"If you got the money," Ron said. He craned to look at the blue-black ceiling, where the lights were arranged to simulate the constellations seen from Rymik, and whistled softly. "I read about places like this but I never thought I'd be in one."

"Wish I could have brought the kids," the Slug mused. "They thought the Baron's was something."

At the alcove the waiter held Mollya's chair.

"Was that Baron Ver Dorco of the War Yards?"

"Yeah," said Calli. "Barbequed lamb, plum wine, the best looking peacocks I've seen in two years. Never got to eat 'em." He shook his head.

"One of the annoying habits of aristocracy," T'mwarba laughed, "they'll go ethnic at the slightest provocation. But there're only a few of us left, and most of us have the good manners to drop our titles."

"Late weapons master of Armsedge," the Slug corrected.

"I read the report of his death. Rydra was there?"

"We all were. It was a 'retty wild evening."

"What exactly happened?"

Brass shook his head. "Well, Ca'tain went early . . ." When he had finished recounting the incidents, with the others adding details, Dr. T'mwarba sat back in his chair.

"The papers didn't give it that way. But they wouldn't. What was this TW-55 anyway?"

Brass shrugged.

There was a click as the discorporaphone in the doctor's ear went on: "It's a human being who's been worked over and over from birth till it isn't human anymore," the Eye said. "I was with Captain Wong when the Baron first showed it to her."

Dr. T'mwarba nodded. "Is there anything else you can tell me?"

Slug, who had been trying to get comfortable in the hardbacked chair, now leaned his stomach against the table edge. "Why?"

The others got still, quickly.

The fat man looked at the rest of the crew. "Why are we telling him all this? He's going back and give it to the stellarmen."

"That's right," Dr. T'mwarba said. "Any of it that might help Rydra."

Ron put down his glass of iced cola. "The stellarmen haven't been what you'd call nice to us, Doc," he explained.

"They don't take us to no fancy restaurants." Calli tucked his napkin into the zircon necklace he'd worn for the occasion. A waiter placed a bowl of french fried potatoes on the table, turned away, and came back with a platter of hamburgers.

Across the table Mollya picked up the tall, red flask and looked at it questioningly.

"Ketchup," Dr. T'mwarba said.

"Ohhh," breathed Mollya and returned it to the damask table cloth.

"Diavalo should be here now." The Slug sat back slowly and stopped looking at the doctor. "He's an artist with a carbo-synth, and he's got a feel for a protein-dispenser that's fine for good solid meals like nut stuffed pheasant, fillet of snapper-meyonaise, and good stick-to-your-ribs food for a hungry spaceship crew. But this fancy stuff"—he spread mustard carefully across his bun—"give him a pound of real chopped meat, and I bet he'd run out of the galley 'cause it might bite him."

Brass said: "What's wrong with Ca'tain Wong? That's what nobody wants to ask."

"I don't know. But if you'll tell me all you can, I'll have a lot better chance of doing something."

"The other thing nobody wants to say," Brass went on, "is that *one* of us don't want you to do anything for her. But we don't know which."

The others silenced again.

"There was a s'y on the shi'. We all knew about it. It tried to destroy the shi' twice. I think it's res'onsible for whatever ha''ened to Ca'tain Wong and the Butcher."

"We all think so," the Slug said.

"This is what you didn't want to tell the stellarmen?" Brass nodded.

"Tell him about the circuit boards and the phony take off before we got to Tarik," Ron said.

Brass explained.

"If it hadn't been for the Butcher," the discorporaphone clicked again, "we would have reentered normal space in the Cygnus Nova. The Butcher convinced Tarik to hook us out and take us aboard."

"So." Dr. T'mwarba looked around the table. "One of you is a spy."

"It could be one of the kids," the Slug said. "It doesn't have to be someone at this table."

"If it is," Dr. T'mwarba said, "I'm talking to the rest of you. General Forester couldn't get anything out of you. Rydra needs somebody's help. It's that simple."

Brass broke the lengthening silence. "I'd just lost a shi' to the Invaders, Doc; a whole 'latoon of kids, more than half the officers. Even though I could wrestle well and was a good 'ilot, to any other trans'ort ca'tain, that run-in with the Invaders made me a stiff jinx. Ca'tain Wong's not from our world. But wherever she came from, she brought a set of values with her that said, 'I like your work and I want to hire you.' I'm grateful."

"She knows about so much," Calli said. "This is the wildest trip I've ever been on. Worlds. That's it, Doc. She cuts through worlds and don't mind taking you along. When's the last time somebody took me to a Baron's for dinner and espionage? Next day I'm eating with pirates. And here I am now. Sure I want to help."

"Calli's too mixed up with his stomach," Ron interrupted. "What it is, is she gets you thinking, Doc. She made me think about Mollya and Calli. You know, she was tripled with Muels Aranlyde, the guy who wrote *Empire Star.* But I guess you must, if you're her doctor. Anyway, you start thinking that maybe those people who live in other worlds—like Calli says—where people write books or make weapons, are real. If you believe in them, you're a little more ready to believe in yourself. And when somebody who can do that needs help, you help."

"Doctor," Mollya said, "I was dead. She made me alive. What can I do?"

"You can tell me everything you know"—he leaned across the table and locked his fingers—"about the Butcher."

"The Butcher?" Brass asked. The others were surprised. "What about him? We don't know anything exce't that Ca'tain and him got to be real close."

"You were on the same ship with him for three weeks. Tell me everything you saw him do."

They looked at one another, silence questioning.

"Was there anything that might have indicated where he was from?"

"Titin," Calli said. "The mark on his arm."

"Before Titin, at least five years before. The problem is that the Butcher doesn't know either."

They looked even more perplexed. Then Brass said, "His language. Ca'tain said he originally had s'oken a language where there was no word for 'I'."

Dr. T'mwarba frowned more deeply as the discorporaphone clicked again. "She taught him how to say *I* and *you*. They wandered through the graveyard in evening, and we hovered over them while they taught each other who they were."

"The 'I'," T'mwarba said, "that's something to go on." He sat back. "It's funny. I suppose I know everything about Rydra there is to know. And I know just that little about ———"

The discorporaphone clicked a third time. "You don't know about the myna bird."

T'mwarba was surprised. "Of course I do. I was there."

The discorporate crew laughed softly. "But she never told you why she was so frightened."

"It was a hysterical onset brought about by her previous condition———"

Ghostly laughter again. "The worm, Dr. T'mwarba. She wasn't afraid of the bird at all. She was afraid of the telepathic impression of a huge worm crawling toward her, the worm that the bird was picturing."

"She told you this———" and never told me, was the ending of what had begun in minor outrage and ceased in wonder.

"Worlds," the ghost reiterated. "Sometimes worlds exist under your eyes and you never see. This room might be filled with phantoms; you never know. Even the rest of the crew can't be sure what we're saying now. But Captain Wong, she never used a discorporaphone. She found a way to talk with us without one. She cut through worlds, and joined them—that's the important part—so that both became bigger."

"Then somebody's got to figure out where in the world,

yours, or mine, or hers, the Butcher came from." A memory
resolved like a cadence closing, and he laughed. The others
looked puzzled. "A worm. *Somewhere in Eden now, a worm,
a worm* . . . That was one of her earliest poems. And it never
occurred to me."

IV

~~~~~~

"Am I supposed to be happy?" Dr. T'mwarba asked.

"You're supposed to be interested," said General Forester.

"You've looked at a hyperstatic map and discovered that
though the sabotage attempts over the last year and a half lie
all over a galaxy in regular space, they're within cruiser
distance of the Specelli Snap across the jump. Also, you've
discovered that during the time the Butcher was in Titin, there
were no 'accidents' at all. In other words, you have discovered
that the Butcher could be responsible for the whole business,
just from physical proximity. No, I am not happy at all."

"Why not?"

"Because he's an important person."

"Important?"

"I know he's . . . important to Rydra. The crew told me
that."

"Him?" Then comprehension struck. *"Him?* Oh, no.
Anything else. He's the lowest form of . . . Not that. Treason,
sabotage, how many murders . . . I mean he's——"

"You don't know what he is. And if he's responsible for
the Babel-17 attacks, in his own right he's as extraordinary as
Rydra." The Doctor stood from his bubble seat. "Now will
you give me a chance to try out my idea? I've been listening
to yours all morning. Mine will probably work."

"I still don't understand what you want, though."

Dr. T'mwarba sighed. "First I want to get Rydra and the Butcher and us in the most heavily guarded, deepest, darkest, impenetrable dungeon Administrative Alliance Headquarters has——"

"But we don't have a dun——"

"Don't put me on," Dr. T'mwarba said evenly. "You're fighting a war, remember?"

The General made a face. "Why all this security?"

"Because of the mayhem this guy has caused up till now. He's not going to enjoy what I plan to do. I'd just be happier if there was something, like the entire military force of the Alliance, on my side. Then I'd feel I had a chance."

Rydra sat on one side of the cell, the Butcher on the other, both strapped to plastic coated chair forms that were part of the walls. Dr. T'mwarba looked after the equipment that was being rolled from the room. "No dungeons and torture chambers, eh, General?" He glanced at a spot of red-brown that had dried on the stone floor by his foot, and shook his head. "I'd be happier if the place was swabbed out with acid and disinfected first. But, I suppose on short order——"

"Do you have all your equipment here, Doctor?" the General asked, ignoring the Doctor's goad. "If you change your mind I can have a barrage of specialists here inside of fifteen minutes."

"The place isn't big enough," Dr. T'mwarba said. "I've got nine specialists right here." He rested his hand on a medium-sized computer that had been placed in the corner beside the rest. "I'd just as soon you weren't here, either. But since you won't go, just watch quietly."

"You say," General Forester said, "you want maximum security. I can have a few two hundred and fifty pound akido masters in here also."

"I have a black belt in akido, General. I think the two of us will do."

The General raised his eyebrows. "I'm karate myself. Akido is one martial art I've never really understood. And you have a black belt?"

Dr. T'mwarba adjusted a larger piece of equipment and nodded. "So does Rydra. I don't know what the Butcher can do, so I'm keeping everybody strapped good and tight."

"Very well." The General touched something at the corner of the door jamb. The metal slab lowered slowly. "We'll be in here five minutes." The slab reached the floor and the line along the edge of the door disappeared. "We're welded in now. We're at the center of twelve layers of defense, all impenetrable. Nobody even knows the location of the place, including myself."

"After those labyrinths we came through, I certainly don't," T'mwarba said.

"Just in case somebody managed to map it, we're moved automatically every fifteen seconds. He's not going to get out." The General gestured toward the Butcher.

"I'm just assuming no one can get in." T'mwarba pressed a switch.

"Go over this once more."

"The Butcher has amnesia, say the doctors on Titin. That means his consciousness is restricted to the section of his brain with synapse connections dating from '61. His consciousness is, in effect, restricted to one segment of his cortex. What this does"—the doctor lifted a metal helmet and put it on the Butcher's head, glancing at Rydra—"is create a series of 'unpleasantnesses' in that segment until he is driven out of that part of the brain back into the rest."

"What if there simply are no connections from one part of the cortex to the other?"

"If it gets unpleasant enough, he will make new ones."

"With the sort of life he's led," commented the General, "I wonder what would be unpleasant enough to drive him out of his head."

"Onoff, Algol, Fortran," said Dr. T'mwarba.

The General watched the doctor make further adjustments. "Ordinarily this would create a snake pit situation in the brain. However, with a mind that doesn't know the word 'I', or hasn't known it for long, fear tactics won't work."

"What will?"

"Algol, Onoff, and Fortran, with the help of a barber and the fact that it's Wednesday."

"Dr. T'mwarba, I didn't bother with more than a precursory check on your psyche-index——"

"I know what I'm doing. None of those computer languages have the word for 'I' either. This prevents such statements as 'I can't solve the problem.' Or, 'I'm really not interested.' Or 'I've got better things to waste my time with.' General, in a little town on the Spanish side of the Pyrenees there is only one barber. This barber shaves all the men in the town who do not shave themselves. Does the barber shave himself or not?"

The General frowned.

'You don't believe me? But General, I always tell the truth. Except Wednesdays; on Wednesday every statement I make is a lie."

"But today's Wednesday!" the General exclaimed, beginning to fluster.

"How convenient. Now, now, General, don't hold your breath until you're blue in the face."

"I'm not holding my breath!"

"I didn't say you were. But just answer yes or no: have you stopped beating your wife?"

"Damn it, I can't answer a question like . . ."

"Well, while you think about your wife, decide whether to hold your breath, bearing in mind that it's Wednesday, tell me: who shaves the barber?"

The General's confusion broke open into laughter. "Paradoxes! You mean you're going to feed him paradoxes he's got to contend with."

"When you do it to a computer, they burn out unless they've been programmed to turn off when confronted with them."

"Suppose he decides to discorporate?"

"Let a little thing like discorporation stop me?" He pointed to another machine. "That's what this is for."

"Just one more thing. How do you know what paradoxes to give him? Surely the ones you told me wouldn't—"

"They wouldn't. Besides, they only exist in English and a few other analytically clumsy languages. Paradoxes break down into linguistic manifestations of the language in which they're expressed. For the Spanish barber, and Wednesday,

it's the words 'every' and 'all' that hold contradictory meanings. The construction 'don't until' has a similar ambiguity.
The same with the word 'stop.' The tape Rydra sent me was a
grammar and vocabulary of Babel-17. Fascinating. It's the
most analytically exact language imaginable. But that's because everything is flexible, and ideas come in huge numbers
of congruent sets, governed by the same words. This just
means that the number of paradoxes you can come up with is
staggering. Rydra had filled the whole last half of the tape up
with some of the more ingenious. If a mind limited to
Babel-17 got caught up in them, it would burn itself out, or
break down——''

"Or escape to the other side of the brain. I see. Well, go
ahead. Start."

"I did two minutes ago."

The General looked at the Butcher. "I don't see anything."

"You won't for another minute." He made a further
adjustment. "The paradoxical system I've set up has to worm
itself through the entire conscious part of his brain. There are
a lot of synapses to start clicking on and off."

Suddenly the lips of the hard muscled face pulled back
from the teeth.

"Here we go," Dr. T'mwarba said.

"What's happening to Miss Wong?"

Rydra's face underwent the same contortion.

"I'd hoped that wouldn't happen," Dr. T'mwarba sighed,
"but I suspected it would. They're in telepathic union."

A *crack* from the Butcher's chair. The headstrap had
been slightly loose and his skull struck the back of his chair.

A sound from Rydra, opening into a full-throated wail
that suddenly choked off. Her startled eyes blinked twice, and
she cried, "Oh, Mocky, it hurts!"

One of the armstraps gave on the Butcher's chair, and
the fist flew up.

Then a light by Dr. T'mwarba's thumb went from white
to amber, and the thumb jammed down on the switch.
Something happened in the Butcher's body; he relaxed.

General Forester started, "He discor——''

But the Butcher was panting.

"Let me out of here, Mocky," came from Rydra.

Dr. T'mwarba brushed his hand across a micro-switch and the bands that had bound her forehead, calves, wrists, and arms came loose with popping sounds. She rushed across the cell to the Butcher. "Him too?"

She nodded.

He pushed the second micro-switch and the Butcher fell forward into her arms. She went down to the floor with his weight, at the same time began working her knuckles along the stiffened muscles on his back.

General Forester was holding a vibra-gun on them. "Now who the hell is he and where is he from?" he demanded.

The Butcher started to collapse again, but his hands slapped the floor and he held himself up. "Ny . . ." he began. "I . . . I'm Nyles Ver Dorco." His voice had lost the grating mineral quality. The pitch was nearly a fourth higher and a slight aristocratic drawl suffused his words. "Armsedge. I was born at Armsedge. And I've . . . I've killed my father!"

The door slab raised into the wall. There was an inrush of smoke and the odor of hot metal. "Now what the devil is that smell?" General Forester said. "That's not supposed to happen."

"I would guess," Dr. T'mwarba said, "the first half dozen layers of defenses for this security chamber have been broken through. Had it taken a few minutes longer, chances are we wouldn't be here."

A rush of footsteps. A soot-streaked stellarman staggered through the door. "General Forester, are you all right? The outer wall exploded, and somehow the radio-locks on the double-gates were shorted out. Something cut halfway through the ceramic walls. It looks like lasers or something."

The General got very pale. "What was trying to get in here?"

Dr. T'mwarba looked at Rydra.

The Butcher got to his feet, holding on to her shoulder. "A couple of my father's more ingenious models, first cousins to TW-55. There are maybe six in inconspicuous, but

effective, positions through the staff here at Administrative
Alliance Headquarters. But you don't have to worry about
them any more."

"Then I'd appreciate it," General Forester said measuredly,
"if you would all get the hell up to my office and explain
what's going on."

"No. My father wasn't a traitor, General. He simply
wanted to make me into the Alliance's most powerful secret
agent. But the weapon is not the tool; rather the knowledge of
how to use it. And the Invaders had that, and that knowledge
is Babel-17."

"All right. You could be Nyles Ver Dorco. But that just
makes a few things I thought I understood an hour ago more
confusing."

"I don't want him to talk too much," Dr. T'mwarba
said. "The strain his whole nervous system has just been
through——"

"I'm all right, Doctor. I've got a complete spare set. My
reflexes are quite above normal and I've got control of my
whole autonomic layout, down to how fast my toenails grow.
My father was a very thorough man."

General Forester swung his boot heel against the front of
his desk. "Better let him go on. Because if I don't understand
this whole business in five minutes, I'll put you all away."

"My father had just begun his work on custom tailored
spies when he got the idea. He had me doctored up into the
most perfect human he could devise. Then he sent me into
Invader territory with the hope I would wreak as much
confusion among them as I could. And I did a lot of damage
too, before they captured me. Another thing Dad realized was
that he would be making rapid progress with the new spies,
and eventually they would far outstrip me—which was quite
true. I didn't hold a candle to TW-55 for example. But
because of—I guess it was family pride, he wanted to keep
control of their operations in the family. Every spy from
Armsedge can receive radio commands through a pre-established
key. Grafted under my medula is a hyperstasis transmitter
most of whose parts are electroplastiplasms. No matter how
complexed the future spies became, I was still in primary

control of the whole fleet of them. Over the past years, several thousand have been released into Invader territory. Up until the time I was captured, we made a very effective force.''

''Why weren't you killed?'' the General asked. ''Or did they find out and manage to turn that entire army of spies back on us?''

''They did discover that I was an Alliance weapon. But that hyperstasis transmitter breaks down under certain conditions and flushes out with my body's waste matter. It takes me about three weeks to grow a new one. So they never learned I was in control of the rest. But they had just come up with their own secret weapon, Babel-17. They gave me a thorough case of amnesia, left me with no communication facilities save Babel-17, then let me escape from Nueva-nueva York back into Alliance territory. I didn't get any instructions to sabotage you. The powers I had, the contact with the other spies dawned on me very painfully and very slowly. And my whole life as a saboteur masquerading as a criminal just grew up. How, or why, I still don't know.''

''I think I can explain that, General,'' Rydra said. ''You can program a computer to make mistakes, and you do it not by crossing wires, but by manipulating the 'language' you teach it to 'think' in. The lack of an 'I' precludes any self-critical process. In fact it cuts out any awareness of the symbolic process at all—which is the way we distinguish between reality and our expression of reality.''

''Come again?''

''Chimpanzees,'' Dr. T'mwarba interrupted, ''are quite coordinated enough to learn to drive cars, and smart enough to distinguish between red and green lights. But once they learn, they still can't be turned loose, because when the light goes green, they will drive through a brick wall if it's in front of them, and if the light turns red, they will stop in the middle of an intersection even if a truck is bearing down on top of them. They don't have the symbolic process. For them, red *is* stop, and green *is* go.''

''Anyway,'' Rydra went on. ''Babel-17 as a language contains a pre-set program for the Butcher to become a criminal and saboteur. If you turn somebody with no memory

loose in a foreign country with only the words for tools and
machine parts, don't be surprised if he ends up a mechanic.
By manipulating his vocabulary properly you can just as
easily make him a sailor, or an artist. Also, Babel-17 is such
an exact analytical language, it almost assures you technical
mastery of any situation you look at. And the lack of an 'I'
blinds you to the fact that though it's a highly useful way to
look at things, it isn't the only way."

"But you mean that this language could even turn you
against the Alliance?" the General asked.

"Well," said Rydra, "to start off with, the word for
Alliance in Babel-17 translates literally into English as:
one-who-has-invaded. You take it from there. It has all sorts
of little diabolisms programmed into it. While thinking in
Babel-17 it becomes perfectly logical to try and destroy your
own ship and then blot out the fact with self-hypnosis so you
won't discover what you're doing and try and stop yourself."

"That's your spy!" Dr. T'mwarba interrupted.

Rydra nodded. "It 'programs' a self-contained schizoid
personality into the mind of whoever learns it, reinforced by
self-hypnosis—which seems the sensible thing to do since
everything else in the language is 'right', whereas any other
tongue seems so clumsy. This 'personality' has the general
desire to destroy the Alliance at any cost, and at the same
time remain hidden from the rest of the consciousness until
it's strong enough to take over. That's what happened to us.
Without the Butcher's pre-capture experience, we weren't
strong enough to keep complete control, although we could
stop them from doing anything destructive."

"Why didn't they completely dominate you?" Dr.
T'mwarba asked.

"They didn't count on my 'talent', Mocky," Rydra said.
"I analyzed it with Babel-17 and it's very simple. The human
nervous system puts out radio noise. But you'd have to have
an antenna of several thousand miles surface area to tune in
anything fine enough to make sense out of that noise. In fact,
the only thing with that sort of area is another human nervous
system. It happens to an extent in everybody. A few people
like me just happen to have better control of it. The schizoid
personalities aren't all that strong, and I've also got some

control of the noise I send out. I've just been jamming
them."

"And what am I supposed to do with these schizy
espionage agents each of you is housing in your head?
Lobotomize you?"

"No," Rydra said. "The way you fix your computer
isn't to hack out half the wires. You correct the language,
introduce the missing elements and compensate for ambiguities."

"We introduced the main elements," the Butcher said,
"back in Tarik's graveyard. We're well on the way to the
rest."

The General stood up slowly. "It won't do." He shook
his head. "T'mwarba, where's that tape?"

"Right in my pocket where it's been since this afternoon,"
Dr. T'mwarba said, pulling out the spool.

"I'm taking this right down to cryptography, then we're
going to start all over again." He walked to the door. "Oh,
yes, and I'm locking you in." He left, and the three looked at
each other.

V

"... yes, of course I should have known that somebody
who could get halfway through to our maximum security
room and sabotage the war effort over one whole arm of the
galaxy could escape from my locked office! ... I am *not* a
nit-wit, but I thought— I know you don't care what I think,
but they— No, it didn't occur to me that they were going to
steal a ship. Well, yes, I— No. Of course I didn't assume—
Yes, it was one of our largest battleships. But they left
a— No, they're not going to attack our— I have *no* way of
knowing except that they left a note saying— Yes, on my
desk, they left a note. . . . Well, of course I'll read it to you.
That's what I've been trying to do for the last . . ."

VI

~~~~~~

Rydra stepped into the spacious cabin of the battleship *Chronos*. Ratt was riding her piggyback.

As she lowered him to the floor, the Butcher turned from the control panel. "How's everybody doing down there?"

"Anybody really confused with the new controls?" Rydra asked.

The platoon boy pulled his ear. "I don't know, Captain. This here is a lot of ship for us to run."

"We just have to get back to the Snap and give this ship to Tarik and the others on Jebel. Brass says he can get us there if you kids keep everything moving smooth."

"We're trying. But there're so many orders all coming through from all over the place at once. I should be down there now."

'You can get down there in a minute," Rydra said. "Suppose I make you honorary quipucamayocuna?"

"Who?"

"That's the guy who reads all the orders as they come through and interprets them and hands them out. Your great grandparents were Indian, weren't they?"

"Yeah. Seminoles."

Rydra shrugged. "Quipucamayocuna is Mayan. Same difference. They gave orders by tying knots in rope; we use punch cards. Scoot, and just keep us flying."

Ratt touched his forehead and scooted.

"What do you think the General made of your note?" the Butcher asked her.

"It doesn't really matter. It will make its round of all the top officials; and they'll ponder over it and the possibility will be semantically imprinted in their minds, which is a good bit of the job. And we have Babel-17 corrected—perhaps I should call it Babel-18—which is the best tool conceivable to build it into truth."

"Plus my battery of assistants," the Butcher said. "I think six months should do it. You're lucky those sickness attacks weren't from the speeded up metabolic rates after all. That sounded a little odd to me. You should have collapsed before you came out of Babel-17, if that was the case."

"It was the schiz-configuration trying to force its way into dominance. Well, as soon as we finish with Tarik, we have a message to leave on the desk of Invader Commander Meihlow at Nueva-nueva York."

"This war will end within six months," she quoted. "Best prose sentence I ever wrote. But now we have to work."

"We have the tools to do it no one else has," the Butcher said. He moved over as she sat beside him. "And with the right tools it shouldn't be too difficult. What are we going to do with our spare time?"

"I'm going to write a poem, I think. But it may be a novel. I have a lot to say."

"But I'm still a criminal. Canceling out bad deeds with good is a linguistic fallacy that's gotten people in trouble more than once. Especially if the good deed is in the offing. I'm still responsible for a lot of murders. To end this war I may have to use dad's spies to make a lot more . . . mistakes. I'll just try to keep them down."

"The whole mechanism of guilt as a deterrent to right action is just as much a linguistic fault. If it bothers you, go back, get tried, be acquitted, then go on about your business. Let me be your business for a while."

"Sure. But who says I get acquitted at this trial?"

Rydra began to laugh. She stopped before him, took his hands, and laid her face against them, still laughing. "But I'll be your defense! And even without Babel-17, you should know by now, I can talk my way out of anything."

—*New York*.
Dec '64—Sept '65

ABOUT THE AUTHOR

Born in 1942, SAMUEL R. DELANY grew up in New York City. His science fiction novels include *The Jewels of Aptor* (1962), a trilogy generally known by its collective title, *The Fall of the Towers* (1963–'64–'65), *Babel-17* (1966), *The Einstein Intersection* (1967), the last two of which won Nebula Awards as best novels of their respective years, and *Nova* (1968). His other books include the bestselling *Dhalgren* (1975), *Triton* (1976), the sword-and-sorcery book, *Tales of Nevèrÿon* (1978) and a beautifully illustrated edition of his SF and fantasy stories, *Distant Stars* (1981). His essays on SF are collected in two volumes, *The Jewel-Hinged Jaw* (1977) and *Starboard Wine* (1982). He has also written an extended essay on urban communes, *Heavenly Breakfast* (Bantam, 1978), and a book-length semiotic study of the SF short story "Angouleme" by Thomas Disch, *The American Shore* (1978). After some years living in Europe and San Francisco and teaching in the Midwest, he again lives in New York.

The World of Samuel R. Delany

Samuel R. Delany is one of science fiction's most insightful and dazzling talents. Winner of the Hugo Award and four-time winner of the Nebula Award, his novels have been hailed by his ever-growing audience and by critics across the country.

"The most interesting author of science fiction writing in English today."

—*New York Times Book Review*

"I can't think of any science fiction writer who possesses more grace and more wisdom than Samuel R. Delany . . . a truly remarkable private vision of the world, unlike anyone else's."

—Frederik Pohl

"As much as any single writer, Samuel R. Delany is responsible for the new themes and techniques that have come to SF since the middle '60s . . . one of the most creative minds in the genre."

—*Newsday*

On the following pages, you will witness some of the many facets of Samuel R. Delany's brilliant, evocative world . . .

DHALGREN
by
Samuel R. Delany

The sun has grown deadly, the world has gone mad. Society has perished, savagery rules over all. All that was known is over, all that was familiar is strange and terrible. Today and yesterday collide with tomorrow. In these dying days of earth, a young drifter enters the city . . .

A towering novel of love and terror at the end of time.

(On sale now wherever Bantam Books are sold.)

NOVA
by
Samuel R. Delany

A passion for vengeance drove Captain Lorq von Ray to dare what no mortal had ever done—to sail through the splintering core of a disintegrating sun.

"As of this book, Samuel R. Delany is the best science fiction writer in the world!"

—*Galaxy*

(On sale now wherever Bantam Books are sold.)

TRITON
by
Samuel R. Delany

The human race has colonized the outer satellites. One of
them is Triton, moon of Neptune, where the ideals of
universal prosperity are possible. Yet Earth threatens war.
Within this strange climate of complete utopia and certain
doom, Bron Helstrom seeks passion and purpose in a
gypsy woman whose wisdom and power will forever re-
verse his life.

All the fascinating color, invention and romance of classic
science fiction in a futuristic novel for today.

TALES OF
NEVÈRŸON
by
Samuel R. Delany

A collection of epic adventures in a realm of fantasy set in the fabulous kingdom of Nevèrÿon, a barbarous empire ruled by primal brutality, intrigue and fear ... a world of bizarre paradoxes, powerful mysteries and sexual abandon.

"The cumulative effect is dazzling."

—*Science Fiction Chronicle*

BABEL-17
by
Samuel R. Delany

*Winner
of the
★ Nebula ★
Award*

A brilliant poet and her colorful crew range the galaxy to solve the riddle of a mysterious battle-code that has become a deadly weapon in the hands of the enemy.

A thrilling adventure of intricate invention.

(On sale now wherever Bantam Books are sold.)

An excerpt from
BABEL-17

A man at the ramp's head had a face like brown rock cut roughly and put together fast. He wore an outdated garment, the sort that had preceded countour capes. It automatically formed to the body, but was made of porous plastic and looked rather like armor. A black, deep piled material cloaked one shoulder and arm. His worn sandals were laced high on his calves. Tufts of fur beneath the thongs prevented chafing. His only cosmetisurgury was false silver hair and upswept metallic eyebrows. From one distended earlobe hung a thick silver ring. He touched his vibra-gun holster resting on his stomach as he looked from hammock to hammock.

A second man stepped in front. He was a slim, fantastic concoction of cosmetisurgical invention, sort of a griffin, sort of a monkey, sort of a sea horse: scales, feathers, claws and beak had been grafted to a body that looked like it originally resembled a cat's. He crouched at the first man's side, squatting on surgically distended haunches, brushing his knuckles on the metal flooring. He glanced up as the first man absently reached down to scratch his head.

Rydra waited for them to speak. A word would release identification: Alliance or Invader. Her mind was ready to spring on whatever tongue they spoke, to extract what she knew of its thinking habits, tendencies toward logical ambiguities, absence or presence of verbal rigor, in whatever areas she might take advantage of—

THE EINSTEIN
INTERSECTION
by
Samuel R. Delany

Winner
★ *of the* ★
Nebula
Award

In the far-distant future, long after humans have left the
Earth, an alien race lives out mankind's oldest myths, and
a young musician seeks his lost love beyond the shores of
death.

At once epic adventure and legend retold, THE EIN-
STEIN INTERSECTION is Delany's most resounding
work.

*(On sale March 15, 1982 wherever Bantam Books are
sold.)*

An excerpt from
THE EINSTEIN INTERSECTION

A roar:

An unmusical sound with much that was metallic in it, neither rage nor pathos, but noise, heaved from lungs bigger than smelting bellows, a long sound, then echoing while the leaves turned up beneath a breeze.

Under green and silver we started again through the cool, dangerous glades.

And step and breathe and step.

Then in the trees to our left—

He came leaping, and that leap rained us with shadow and twigs and bits of leaf.

Turning his haunch with one foreleg over here and hindleg *way* the hell over there, he looked down at us with an eye bloodshot, brown and thickly oystered in the corners. His eyeball must have been big as my head.

The wet, black nostrils steamed.

He was very noble.

Then he tossed his head, breaking branches, and hunkered with his fists punched into the ground—there were hands with horny hairy fingers thick as my arm where he should have had forehooves—bellowed, reared, and sprang away.

THE JEWELS OF APTOR
by
Samuel R. Delany

Filled with rich poetry and vivid imagery, Samuel R. Delany's first novel is the story of a poet, a thief and a bear-like giant who follow a triple goddess to a ruined land ruled by monsters in search of gems of unimaginable power.

"Outrageously fantastic, romantic . . . full of bits and glimpses of bizarre beauty . . . with a denoument that lifts the story out of itself."

—*Analog*

(On sale May 15, 1982 wherever Bantam Books are sold.)

An excerpt from
THE JEWELS OF APTOR

The shapes dropped like foundering kites: sixty feet above them, forty feet, thirty. There was a piercing shriek. Geo was up on his feet, and Iimmi beside him, their staffs in hand. The shadows fell, shrieking; wings began to flap violently, and they rose again, moving out from the wall. Now they turned back.

Twenty feet away they hit the ground, black wings crumpling in the moonlight. In the growing horde of shadow, light snagged on a metal blade.

Two of the creatures detached themselves from the others and hurled themselves forward, swords arcing suddenly above their heads in silver light.

Urson grabbed Geo's staff and swung it as hard as he could, catching both beasts on the chest. They fell backwards in an explosion of rubbery wings, as though they had stumbled into sheets of dark canvas.

Three more leaped the fallen ones, shrieking. As they came, Urson looked up and jammed his staff into the belly of a fourth monster about to fall on them from above. One got past Iimmi's whistling staff and Geo grabbed a furry arm. He pulled it to the side, over-balancing the sailed creature. It dropped its sword as it lay for a moment, struggling on its back. Geo snatched the blade and brought it up from the ground into the gut of another of the creatures who spread its wings and staggered back. He yanked the blade free, and turned it down into the body of the fallen one; it made a sound like a suddenly crushed sponge.

THE BALLAD OF BETA-2
by
Samuel R. Delany

In the ruined hulks of the Star Folk's fleet, Joneny, a student of galactic lore, seeks the answer to a riddle posed by a long-forgotten ballad. What Joneny learns unleashes an awesome force on the galaxy.

(On sale July 15, 1982 wherever Bantam Books are sold.)

An excerpt from
THE BALLAD OF BETA-2

Joneny lowered the view-pointer until he seemed to be standing on the hull. Then he looked around.

The horizon was frighteningly close and the plates which he had expected to be smooth and even looked like gnawed cheese: they were rotten, crystallized into ruts and flaking mounds, green with a color of their own, deeper than the light lent by the far sun. He looked up.

And stopped breathing. Fourteen times the size of the appearance of the moon from Earth, hung the Sigma-9. He knew that nothing moved in this stasis. He knew he was safely in his ship, minutes away from a dozen stars and their safe planets. Yet the looming, gutted wreck seemed to be careening toward him through the blackness.

He screamed, threw one hand over his eyes and jammed the other against the mobile vision switch. Quivering, he was back in his ship; the view screen was only a six foot window in front of him once more.

THE FALL OF THE TOWERS
by
Samuel R. Delany

Out of the ashes of the Great Fire arose the mighty empire of Toromon, poised to war against an evil entity from across space called *The Lord of the Flames*. Jón Koshar, fugitive and heir to a great fortune, and a handful of improbable allies must find a way to stop the war.

OUT OF THE DEAD CITY * THE TOWERS OF TORON * CITY OF A THOUSAND SUNS, Samuel R. Delany's monumental trilogy now in one volume.

(On sale September 15, 1982 wherever Bantam Books are sold.)

An excerpt from
THE FALL OF THE TOWERS

The green of beetle's wings . . . the red of polished car-
buncle . . . a web of silver fire. Lightning tore his eyes
apart, struck deep inside his body. He felt his bones split
and clutched the stomach of his coveralls, doubling around
what would be pain. But it was gone. He was falling
through blue smoke, cool as blown ice.

He put his hands out to catch——

Palms and knees scudded in something hot. Jon
Koshar shook his head, looked up. Sand saddled away
from him. His black hair fell over his eyes again; he shook
it away and sat back on his heels.

The sky was turquoise. The horizon was too close.
The sand was more like lime. He looked down. Two
shadows fanned from his body. To his left a tooth of
rock also cast a double shadow.

He staggered erect. He was too light; gravity was all
wrong. The sand burned his toes. Sweat started on the
back of his neck, beneath his arms. The air stung his nasal
cavity. Jon squinted.

Far down the sand was a lake; rising by, or perhaps
from it was a . . . city? He narrowed his eyes more,
staring . . .

Jerk a man from one world; fling him into another.
It will take him the same time to realize where he is as to
remember where he has been. Each location defines the
other.

DISTANT STARS
by
Samuel R. Delany

New fiction, a short novel, vintage stories and a fascinating new essay, with over sixty pages of illustrations, including the first computer-enhanced artwork created for a science fiction book.

Included in this brilliant collection are *Omegahelm* (a new story set in the universe of Delany's forthcoming novel STARS IN MY POCKET LIKE GRAINS OF SAND), the Nebula Award-winning *Time Considered as a Helix of Semi-Precious Stones* and more.

He's a tough-guy detective living in a seedy 21st century America. He smokes hard and drinks hard and is certainly no soft touch when it comes to the ladies. More often than not, he's smack in the middle of danger —but he thinks on his feet and has a great nose for snooping. Catch Mathew Swain in his first three futuristic adventures:

HOT TIME IN OLD TOWN

When someone ices one of Swain's friends, Swain sets out to nail the killer. His relentless thirst for justice takes him to Old Town, a radiation-soaked mutant enclave where Swain uncovers a secret so deadly it's been paid for with a thousand lives. (#14811-7 • $2.25)

WHEN TROUBLE BECKONS (*on sale October 15, 1981*)

When Swain's rich friend Ginny Teal asks Swain to visit her on the moon, he's awfully reluctant. But Ginny sounds desperate and Swain gives in. But when he gets to the Moon, Swain finds Ginny out cold on the floor next to a dead body. (#20041-0 • $2.25)

THE DEADLIEST SHOW IN TOWN (*on sale February 15, 1981*)

Swain is hired for more money than he's worth to find a missing #1 newswoman and plunges deep into the dazzling world of a big video network, a ratings war and the misty borderline between reality and illusion that makes up the video of tomorrow. (#20186-7 • $2.25)

Read all three of these exciting Mathew Swain novels, available wherever Bantam paperbacks are sold.

OUT OF THIS WORLD!

That's the only way to describe Bantam's great series of science fiction classics. These space-age thrillers are filled with terror, fancy and adventure and written by America's most renowned writers of science fiction. Welcome to outer space and have a good trip!

FANTASY AND SCIENCE FICTION FAVORITES

Bantam brings you the recognized classics as well as the current favorites in fantasy and science fiction. Here you will find the beloved Conan books along with recent titles by the most respected authors in the genre.

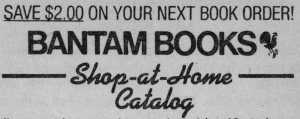